"You and I have been destined to be lovers for years."

Meriel wanted to tell him she was no longer eighteen and vulnerable, but speech was beyond her.

"You are ready for me," Ramon continued thickly. "I will not allow you to leave."

"I—I won't stay here," she stammered. "I won't become—become your mistress!"

"You imagine I need a bedmate only, some pliant toy in my hands?" Ramon smiled, his own arrogance flaring. "If I did, you would come to me. But that is not what I want from you. Your name will be Ortiga, my name. You will be the mother of my children. You are to be my wife. I do not intend to wait any longer. You belong to me and I am claiming you."

The manner of Ramon's speech frightened Merry. He hadn't declared any love for her. He had stated his desire and his intentions, and she was expected to obey.

PATRICIA WILSON used to live in Yorkshire, England, but with her children all grown up, she decided to give up her teaching position there and accompany her husband on an extended trip to Spain. Their travels are providing her with plenty of inspiration for her romance writing.

Books by Patricia Wilson

HARLEQUIN PRESENTS
934—THE FINAL PRICE
1062—A LINGERING MELODY

HARLEQUIN ROMANCE
2856—BRIDE OF DIAZ

PATRICIA WILSON

the ortiga marriage

Harlequin Books

TORONTO • NEW YORK • LONDON
AMSTERDAM • PARIS • SYDNEY • HAMBURG
STOCKHOLM • ATHENS • TOKYO • MILAN

Harlequin Presents first edition June 1988
ISBN 0-373-11086-3

Original hardcover edition published in 1987
by Mills & Boon Limited

CHAPTER ONE

'TELEPHONE call for you, Miss Curtis!'

The voice came clearly to Meriel as she crossed the foyer of the Mackensie Building and she raised a hand in acknowledgement, hurrying on and into the lift.

'Hold it, will you? I'll take it as soon as I reach my office.'

'Right, Miss Curtis. It's an overseas call.'

Meriel nodded pleasantly as the lift doors swished closed and the silent speed lifted her to her third-floor office. Overseas. That would be the call from France. She had been almost certain that she had got the Paris contract and they had promised to ring today if the news was good. Stewart Mackensie was going to have to eat his hat after all. She grinned to herself, looking forward to the next few minutes, cherishing the moment when she could take the lift back down and walk into his office in a casual manner with the news.

Her floor reached, she walked quickly along to her office, her long legs closing the gap between the lift and her own office door with easy, swinging steps, her slender height perfectly balanced. The cap of thick, blonde hair cut in a loose pageboy style swung too as she walked and there was nothing but pleasure on her flawlessly beautiful face. The Paris contract! The biggest thing she had pulled off yet!

'All right, Sandra. I've arrived.'

'Yes, Miss Curtis. Your call from Venezuela, Miss Curtis.' The telephonist slid into her professional voice as the line was connected but Meriel froze into icy stillness.

'Meriel?' She didn't answer. She couldn't answer. She had been expecting to hear a French voice, her mind

5

attuned to it, and everything inside her chilled at the deep voice, the softly spoken Spanish sound of her name. For one blinding second, the room dimmed, fading to almost nothing.

'Meriel!' No question now, a command, his natural attitude to life. 'I will assume that you are there but if you do not intend to reply, have the courtesy to replace the receiver. I do not have all the time in the world to listen to empty miles of space!'

Meriel sank into her seat, her mouth dry. Seconds before she had been smiling, her world filled with promise, and now she was shaking, stricken, unable to breathe as the voice of Ramón Ortiga struck out at her from half-way across the world.

'I'm here.' She managed it with no stammers, no hesitation, no sign of fear. 'I was expecting a call from Paris; the change of direction and language stunned me for a second. I had to re-orientate my mind from business.'

'I am well aware of your importance in the world of the Mackensie Press,' he said coldly. 'I am phoning you because it is necessary. Your call from Paris will have to wait.'

Her hand gripped the receiver so hard that she doubted her ability to relax her fingers. Why didn't she simply put the phone down? Why did she sit here with her heart hammering in a panic as she listened to the sound of a voice she had thought never to hear again? The arrogance of his family came across the miles and she could imagine his face, cold, aristocratic, handsome and unbending. She could see again the dark, dark eyes that could flash with fire and narrow to glittering points of anger. She could see the tall, lean, athletic frame leaning indolently against the huge shining desk in his study and it took every bit of her considerable spirit to get a grip on her feelings, to realise that she was free of the Ortiga domination, had been free of it for years.

'Then as you are paying for this expensive and so far

pointless call, may I suggest that you proceed with it?' she said coolly. 'My call from Paris will no doubt be received when this line is clear, therefore, to save you expense and me irritation, please come to the point of your call.'

There was a silence and she could imagine his raised eyebrows. He had always done that when she had answered back, not that she had answered back very often, but when her nerve had been up to it and she had defended herself his attitude had always been one of aloof surprise, raised black brows, a wryly amused twist to his lips. Hatred shot through her like a searing flame and she forestalled his reply.

'I am waiting! I also do not have all the time in the world to listen to empty miles of space, Señor Ortiga!'

'*Por Diós!*' he snapped in an unexpected burst of temper. 'I have been Ramón to you for many years of your life; has your lengthy stay with your own countrymen robbed you of any little courtesy we were able to force into you? I am your stepbrother!'

'You are nothing.' Merial answered flatly, her voice empty of emotion. 'You are a man who is ringing me from Venezuela, criticising me for my conduct. Your right to do that ended long ago when you told me to get back to my own kind. I am with my own kind, with my own countrymen, and you no longer have any right to call me to order. Unless you come to the substance of this call, I shall replace the receiver as you at first suggested. I am expecting an important call and I am at work. I do not have time to conduct a transatlantic battle, nor do I have the interest.'

She stopped speaking and her eyes caught sight of her reflection in the facing mirror. Her face was white and strained, her eyes haunted and she could hear the sound of her own heart.

'Meriel.' He paused and she strained her ears to ascertain if what she had thought was correct. His voice had softened, dropped to a low murmur as she remembered it could do.

'Meriel—you must come home.'

'I am home! I live here, work here. Everything that I . . .'

'Meriel!' The sharp command cut into her heated reply leaving her no further chance to talk. 'There has been an accident. Your mother and my father were in a plane crash. For the love of God do not say anything more! Do not continue with your fight now from so far away, saying words that you will later regret.' He paused and she was so stunned that she could not think of any words at all. The news would just not sink in. 'Come home, Meriel. Now!'

'My mother! Where is she? How are they? Ramón!'

The poignant cry was completely out of the past. The office and her importance, the security of her life in England faded away and she was back in the land where she had spent her childhood years. She was calling his name with the same despairing urgency.

'They are dead, both of them. There is no other way to tell you except in this way. One sharp blow is better than an endless sawing away at the heart.'

There was just the tiniest hint of compassion in the deep, proud voice but Meriel barely heard it. She could see the beautiful, cold face of her mother, the proud and indifferent face of her stepfather, and though she had thought at one time that she would never want to see them again, the realisation that now she never would hit her like a hammer blow.

'You are all right?' Ramón's voice pulled her back in time and she took a deep steadying breath, closing her eyes for a minute but failing to blot out the bitter memories.

'Yes, I'm all right. I'll come at once. When is the funeral?'

'The funeral was this morning.'

She gasped aloud at the even statement, colour from shock and disbelief flooding her face.

'You—you dare to tell me that you held a funeral for my mother—my mother—and I was not informed?'

'In the first place,' he interrupted angrily, 'I had no address, finding you has not been easy. In the second place, I would not have told you even if I had been able to discover your whereabouts in time. I did not want you at the funeral!'

Cold grief flooded over her. Even now, when this tragedy had struck both their lives, he did not want her there.

'Then there is no point whatever in my coming now,' she said unevenly.

'I thought that you would perhaps want to see the place where they are buried,' he informed her quietly. 'But even that is not the point of my call. The dead are dead, it is the living that should concern us both. You have a brother, Meriel, or had you forgotten about Manuel?'

She had. For one small selfish moment she had forgotten Manolito, her dearly loved half-brother, and for the first time, tears flooded her eyes and she was unable to reply. Of course he took her silence to be guilt and continued accordingly.

'Now that you have been reminded,' he rasped, 'let me also remind you that he is here, right in the thick of things. He sees an empty house, he saw the crash and he will not be comforted. He grieves constantly and there is nothing that I can do to reach him. To all my approaches he has but one reply, "I want Merry." It is your duty to return to Venezuela. It is your duty to come home. I am aware that you dislike me for being what I am but our mutual differences must be put aside. Manuel needs you.'

'I'll come.' She almost whispered the words but apparently he heard her because she also heard him as his breath left him in an audible sigh. No wonder he wanted her there; he had resented Manolito as much as he had resented his half-English stepsister, and now he was calling for help when he could not longer cope. She was too stunned by the news and by her words with Ramón to have the energy to say more than, 'I'll get my affairs in order and be out on the first available flight.'

'There is a first-class ticket already waiting for you at the airline office in London. It has no specific date. Make your arrangements with them and then call me. Remember though, that your duty lies here and not with some glossy magazine chain. Manolito is waiting for you. I will be waiting too.'

It sounded like a threat but she was quite used to that, and to the finality of his voice as he replaced the receiver at his end. It was only later that it dawned on her that he had said 'Manolito' and she knew that it was either a slip of the tongue or a sop to induce her to hurry. Ramón Ortiga was not given to calling anyone by a pet name. He was cold all the way through, as cold as the snow on the Andes, as deep and silent as the great stretch of the plains where he had spent his life. It was only her years away from him that gave her the courage to face him again, that and the knowledge that Manolito needed her and was now living in a house without comfort, living in a great *hacienda* with nothing but miles of empty grassland to reach out to.

The call from Paris came almost as soon as Ramón had rung off and she had got the contract, though how she answered the questions, made the arrangements, she was not later able to remember. Her face was still deathly pale, her hands shaking when she took the lift down to Stewart Mackensie's office.

He was on the phone, barely glancing at her as she came in. A great hulk of a man, kind and generous with the faint burr of the Highlands in his voice, he was almost as fair as she was herself. Fair-haired and blue-eyed, the very opposite of Ramón Ortiga. She had often thought guiltily that it was this sharp contrast that had drawn her towards him.

He had taken over the large and thriving chain of

magazines when he was only twenty-six. With no father to take up the flag he had been given little choice when his grandfather, the founder of the Mackensie Press, had died. Under Stewart though the firm had expanded and become very powerful. He often said that he had printing ink in his veins where others merely had blood, and as head of advertising for the whole chain, Meriel knew his worth both as a man and as head of the firm.

Many times he had asked her to marry him but her constant refusals had marred neither their happy working relationship nor their deep friendship.

'All right, you didn't get the advertising contract with Paris, so I don't have to get a straw hat to eat,' he remarked in amusement as he turned from the phone. 'I know you've not got it or you'd have been bouncing about with impatience while I was phoning instead of standing there quietly like . . .'

His voice faded away as he saw her face and he was beside her quickly.

'Meriel! What is it my dear?'

'I got the contract,' she assured him in a small faraway voice, 'the details are here, but somebody else will have to do it. I've got to have leave.' She raised stricken eyes to his and then burst out, 'Oh Stewart! My mother was killed! She's dead! And Ramón said . . . Ramón said . . .' She burst into tears and he folded her against the hard warmth of his chest.

'Hush! Hush!' he said quietly. 'You'll have all the leave you need. What did that stepbrother of yours say?' he added on a rising note of anger.

Meriel told him later over an early drink in a nearby cocktail bar and his face darkened with anger. Over the years that she had known him, the details of her life in Venezuela had come out a little at a time and he was too protective of her to have any sympathy for Ortiga.

'Why the hell can't he fly Manuel out to London?' he

grated. 'The boy will recover a lot more rapidly in a new place.'

'How can he?' she asked simply. 'How can he ask a child to fly at all, let alone so far when his parents have just died in an air crash? Anyway,' she added almost absently, 'he would never let Manuel come to me and leave Venezuela. Manuel is an Ortiga, part of a straight, pure line from the past. There's the inheritance.'

'The bloody inheritance!' Stewart rasped. 'Ortiga seems to be more like a sack of gold than a man, more like a damned golden statue!'

No, she thought tiredly, looking at Stewart but seeing another face, a proud, magnificent face with eyes like jet in the sunlight, a perfect physique that was power, grace and endurance. A body that could rise at dawn and ride with the men until nightfall with no sign of weariness. Not a golden statue, a bronze statue, beautiful to see but cold, cold, cold and cruelly hard.

She didn't speak her thoughts aloud though; instead she said quietly, 'He believes in duty.'

'From what you've told me,' Stewart said in disgust, 'he hasn't a kindly thought in his head. Of course, you'll have to go, my dear, but watch your step. There's no need to take any insults or lordly behaviour from Ortiga. You don't rely on him at all. You're a success in your own right and I'm always here, you know that, Meriel.'

She knew that. She smiled up at him tremulously as his hand covered hers, nodding her agreement, too full of emotion at the moment to say more. Over the years, he had pieced together some of her life in Venezuela, but there was much that she had never spoken of, would never speak of. Stewart Mackensie thought Ramón cruel, but he did not know Ramón. She often thought that she was the only one who knew him, who knew the different expressions that crossed that dark, handsome face. Only she knew that the stern and unbending face of Spanish aristocracy could suddenly melt into the ready laughter of a Venezuelan. Only she knew that the gulf between them was too painful and too deep for any bridge ever to cross.

She was a success. From a painfully insecure, tongue-tied child she had grown into a person with a ready charm that was attractive and persuasive. She had learned the hard way to hide her feelings and talk easily. She could charm birds from trees, according to Stewart, and she had charmed plenty of advertising business their way. Already bilingual, she had taken French and German at school and had used her language skills to draw business from the Continent, and she had climbed fast in the firm.

It was ironic that at the peak of her success, when she had everything she wanted, Ramón should have the power to call her back. No doubt he was no more looking forward to this than she was, but he had ordered her 'home' and she had no alternative but to obey. Once, she had not wanted a career, success, she had wanted only Ramón. Stewart did not know that, only she knew—and Ramón, although he would probably not even remember. Six years was a long time ago, a lifetime ago, it seemed. She had pushed the thought of him away with all the other hurts that she had suffered and she had thought him too distant to hurt her ever again. She had been wrong.

The *llanos*! It would be still dry, parched, waiting for the wet season that began in April. It was mid-March now and even from the air, Meriel could see the tall, coarse grasses of the plains, the leafless trees, the whole of the savanna waiting with a kind of breathless stillness for the torrential rain and the sudden floods that would encourage life and greenery.

The cattle were dotted about the land, small groups of them moving restlessly and worriedly as the light aircraft sped low and noisily above them, but even they seemed too taken up with the breathless waiting to run in any kind of panic. They would soon be gathered into huge herds and moved to higher ground, away from the devastation of floods and the terror of the storms that would sweep the hot dry grasslands that were the *llanos*.

Meriel had watched this scene so often in her life. She had watched it with the same mixture of feelings that flooded through her now. A feeling of relief to see again the wide sweep of the grasslands and the seemingly endless stretch of land and sky, but a tight anxiety within her at what she would face at the grand *hacienda* of the Ortigas.

She cast a swift glance at the broad face and shock of black, curly hair of the man beside her. How many times had Luis Silva flown her across this landscape? How many times had he met her plane at Caracas and led her with wide smiles to the small Ortiga plane that would take her home? How many times too had Ramón waited by the airstrip on the Ortiga ranch to drive her to the cool and indifferent greeting of her mother and stepfather as she had come from boarding school in England to spend the long holidays with her family in Venezuela?

She could not even begin to count the times. It seemed that the whole of her past life had been here, that she had waited always as she waited now for a sight of the tall, dark figure who would be leaning against the station-wagon and who would stare at her coolly as he had always done, assessing, probing, watchful before taking her case and coldly kissing her cheek.

Meriel could see herself as she had been then, slim and uncomfortable, almost too thin, her hair almost invariably wild and windswept, her grey eyes wide and anxious, waiting with almost tearful anxiety for any sign that her appearance displeased Ramón, because she had learned at a very early age that the cold, handsome face of her stepbrother meant either despair or a kind of happiness. Ramón was the only one at the great house who would ever defend her and only his presence gave her any kind of security.

She was neither thin nor windswept now, however, she was grown up, no longer an anxious child. Only the wide grey eyes were the same. Her slender height was not ungainly now, her figure was a woman's figure, smooth-hipped and high-breasted, and her golden hair was smooth and groomed, her make-up as perfect as she could make it. She would not now be meeting her stepbrother in anxiety, watching for any sign of his approval. In any case, she knew now that there would be none, she had known that for almost seven years. As a child she had been vaguely bearable, as a person she was utterly unacceptable.

'At last you are back home on the *llanos*, Señorita Meriel.'

The grating sound of the pilot's voice cut into her thoughts and she met his smile with one of her own.

'For a very little while only, Luis,' she told him softly.

'I am sorry about . . . We are all sorry that you are here because of your great tragedy.' He began hesitantly but she waved his sympathy away gently.

'Thank you, but I'll recover from it.' She forced a smile and moved her hand to take in the great sweep of the plains. 'It is still the same, unchanging, unending.'

'*Sí*, it remains the same, it can do little else.' His dark eyes were suddenly dancing. 'You are changed though, Señorita Meriel. You are—grown up—different.' His dark, laughing eyes skimmed over her and she gave him an answering grin.

'*Sí*, Luis. I am grown up and different. Also I have a very sharp tongue and a nasty turn of phrase.'

'I'll try to remember, *señorita*,' he assured her, bursting into pleased and mischievous laughter. 'I hope that Señor Ortiga remembers too. I have often in the past heard his criticisms of you. You will tell him now where to go?'

'Yes,' she answered flatly. She would. She was not going to be at the mercy of Ramón's tongue ever again, at the first sign of any criticism, any temper, any orders she would . . .

Her thoughts died away in her mind just as her words would have died on her tongue had she been speaking, because he was there. The plane had been steadily losing height as they had talked and now it swooped low over the small dry airstrip to turn and come in with the wind. Ramón was there just as he had always been, just as if this were so many years ago.

She could see him clearly, tall and lithe, leaning against the car, blue jeans moulded to his long strong legs, a blue checked shirt open at the bronze of his neck, his dark eyes narrowed against the sun as he looked up.

God! He was still the same! Her heartbeat changed like an instrument that moves to the rhythm of a remembered song, her skin tightened on her face and tiny pinpricks of alarm raced down the backs of her arms and hands. She was grateful for this advance warning, grateful for the chance to grasp her racing feelings and pull herself together. He could not see her as clearly as she saw him. She too had waited often for the arrival of the plane and she knew that to him she would be little more than a blur, a hazy impression.

She took deep, steadying breaths and won her small battle. As the plane landed she was in control of herself, the knowledge that there must be no sign of weakness when she met Ramón Ortiga bolstering up her courage and stiffening her resolve.

Luis taxied the plane in close with the expertise of many years of practice. The wing was almost over the car before he stopped the engine and turned to her with a grin.

'We are here, *señorita*. Welcome back to the *llanos*.'

'Thank you, Luis. Thank you too for a very pleasant flight. Before too long you will be taking me back to Caracas, a few days at the most I expect.' He nodded but didn't seem too impressed with her plans.

'I am at your service, Señorita Meriel. Whenever you

wish, or whenever Señor Ortiga wishes,' he added softly, his dark eyes twinkling. He grinned widely as she opened her mouth to make a sharp comment and shook his head.

'We had better get out before his temper surfaces, I think.'

He lowered the steps and she moved, waiting for no assistance, but she was a little too late. As she stepped down, strong hands came to her waist and she was lifted the rest of the way and found herself turning pale-faced to meet the dark watchful eyes of her stepbrother.

'Welcome home,' the deep voice said wryly. 'I was beginning to think that you had decided to stay in the plane and return to Caracas.'

'Hardly,' she said coldly. 'I do know my duty after all.'

'Yes,' he countered, 'when you have been reminded of it. Now that you have renewed your acquaintance with Luis perhaps we could go?'

Her grey eyes met the dark eyes of Luis Silva as he came back from putting her luggage in the car and she saw the rueful, 'I told you so' written across his face. She had been met with criticism as usual but her sharp tongue and nasty turn of phrase that she had boasted of seemed at this moment to have deserted her. For the time being she could think of nothing to say to Ramón, as he continued to hold her lightly but firmly by the waist.

'A good idea,' she said flatly. 'The sooner I see Manolito the better and the sooner he is well and recovered the better too. I am too busy to linger for long in this place.'

She pulled away and turned to the car, suddenly annoyed that he had brought the old station-wagon, dusty and dented as usual.

'Why do you continue to drive this contraption when you're knee deep in money?' she said crossly. 'It's uncomfortable, ugly and bone-breaking.'

Evidently, the Venezuelan side of him was uppermost today because he grinned as he slid in beside her.

'You imagine that after seven years it is the same one?'

'It looks the same to me. Dirty, scratched and dented.'

'It is, I think, the fourth,' he assured her quietly. 'I realise that it is not a thing of beauty but it is essential for the work that it does. It is a rough ride to the *hacienda* and I have the choice of this or a Land Rover. I prefer this. I do not like change. The dents may be familiar but they are quite new, I assure you.'

'It's filthy!' she said crossly, drawing the skirt of her green silk dress around her.

'I remember when you were only too happy to see it,' he said softly. 'I remember when you leaned out at the side and let the wind blow your hair into a greater state of wildness. You never complained then.'

'I was too young to recognise discomfort,' she reminded him tartly, 'and I am no longer wild.'

'That I can see, *pequeña*,' he commented wryly, his eyes leaving the track and skimming over her face and figure. 'Your hair is controlled at last.'

'I am also controlled!' she said sharply. 'And I am not a little girl either,' she added in a tight voice, her face flushing at his small but well remembered endearment.

'I can see that too,' he told her softly, lapsing into silence as he normally did when he had said everything that he intended. He was not a man to hold pointless conversations and she could tell after a quick glance at his face that he was slipping back into his usual aloof manner, the burst of humour over.

Meriel clenched her hands and kept silent too. Not one word had he said about her mother, not one word of explanation about his outrageous conduct in barring her from the funeral. She was here because he needed her help, here because he could not cope with Manolito. No doubt he would never recover from the astonishment that the realisation of that had brought. No doubt he would not even have bothered to inform her of the accident and her mother's death if he had been able to cope with Manuel as he coped so coolly with everything else. The bottled-up anger grew and exploded into words when they had gone only a very little way.

'I hate you, Ramón! Do you know that? I hate you!'

'I know it.' He never ever looked at her, keeping his eyes on the difficult track, his hands dark and capable on the wheel.

'You suffer from no remorse, do you?' she stormed on. 'You have not one bit of regret in you that you failed to get me here for the funeral.'

'No.' Short and to the point, his answer drove her further.

'You didn't want me here because I don't fit in, because I'm not an Ortiga. No doubt I would have been an embarrassment at such a gathering as a funeral where my blonde hair and my inability to keep a cold straight face would have stood out so oddly beside the Ortigas!'

'*Diós!*' He stood on the brakes, almost throwing her into the windscreen, and he had his hands tightly and cruelly on her arms before she could recover. 'No,' he rasped brutally. 'I did not want you there! I did not want you to be brought to Venezuela in time to see the remains of the plane, a thousand pieces strewn across the savanna! I did not want you to be on hand for the necessary identification! Have you any idea what it is like when a small plane crashes at speed? Have you, Meriel?' He shook her, his lips tight and angry, and the picture he painted with such cruel words swam into her mind.

'Oh, God!' She was suddenly sick inside, nausea washing over her as she struggled out of the car to lean against the dusty side, her head in her hands, glad to feel the hot wind blowing at her face and hair.

The nausea passed and she let the deep sobs of shock and grief that welled up inside come to the surface. Turning away to face the dusty landscape and hide her face from his she sobbed quietly, racked with pain and unhappiness. It was only in the last few years that she had made any sort of peace with her mother, had had any chance of meeting her on equal terms, and her only comfort was that. Now, she would never see her again, and the ghost of the cruel past would roam through the *hacienda* with very little to remember that was good.

'Stop! Hush! Hush!' Ramón was beside her silently and swiftly, pulling her into his arms. 'You will make yourself ill and it will do no good.'

'I—I'm sorry.' She struggled weakly but he held her fast, his hand smoothing her hair in an oddly comforting gesture that threw her far back into the past. 'I should have realised that . . . Did Manolito go to the funeral?'

'Of course not,' he assured her quietly. 'He is a child. I would not let him suffer anything like that. For the time, I forgot that you were no longer a child. I tried to protect you from the—misery of it all.' He sighed and released her. 'I did not do the right thing I suppose but I saw you still as a girl. You are a woman and well able to face things. 'I suppose I had forgotten. It has been such a long time since . . .'

He turned away and looked out across the tall, dry grassland, his dark eyes shuttered and cool.

'I'm sorry, Ramón,' Meriel whispered. 'I should not have said all that. Sometimes, my tongue runs away with me and—and I suppose that I'm a little bitter.'

He turned to look down at her, much taller than she although she was not in any way small. For a few seconds, their eyes held and communicated without words and her face lost its pale grief and flooded with colour.

'Bitter? Yes, I suppose so,' he said in an odd voice. 'However, you are here, and there is Manuel.'

'Yes.' She bowed her head, ashamed of her outburst, ashamed that she had once again shown her inability to keep calm and indifferent to circumstances. Once again too she had thought of her own grief and only belatedly of Manolito. Ramón had thought of them both.

She was startled to feel his hands on her arms again and looked up into dark unreadable eyes. For a second he stared down into her face and then bent his head, kissing her lightly on the lips.

'Do not let your conscience trouble you so very much, Meriel,' he said softly. 'You always did have more feelings than common sense.'

He turned back to the car and she followed, suddenly very weary and defeated. She was not an Ortiga. An Ortiga would have dealt with any problem coolly and systematically. She was her father's daughter, more English than Spanish, more emotional than sensible, countenanced but unacceptable.

'Once more you are windswept, *pequeña*,' he said softly and she lifted startled eyes to see him waiting with the car door open, an amused quirk to his lips as she hastily tried to straighten the unruliness of her bright hair.

CHAPTER TWO

THE *hacienda* was built on high ground, on the crest of a flat-topped hill. The floods that often swept the plains could never reach it and it had stood for centuries secure and cool, an oasis in a landscape of high, dry grasses, a fortress surrounded by greenery.

The rough stonework of the rambling house was mellow in the afternoon sunlight, the green, well watered lawns stretching out to the wide perimeter walls. It had withstood upheaval and conflict and the ravages of time and weather with the same fortitude that had been in the blood of the first Ortigas who had settled here from Spain and set up the line that was to continue unbroken.

From far away, Meriel saw it. As far as she knew it had never been given any name. To the riders and the workers it was simply the *hacienda*. To the Ortigas it was *la casa* or just home, for although their wealth was drawn from mining, oil and many other sources it was to this place that they returned, it was from the ornate polished desk in the dark study that the Ortiga wealth was controlled.

She remembered her first frightened and awestruck glimpse of the place when she had seen it as a child, a shy and unhappy eleven-year-old. For two years she had been at the centre of a battle as her Spanish-born mother and her English father had fought for custody of her, and Inez had won. She was cool and beautiful, and her calm manner, her aristocratic bearing had finally swayed the court. Her father had been too heated, too impassioned, leaving them with an impression of instability, making his statement that Inez had not one ounce of love in her for the child seem like the ravings of a hysterical mind. His love and compassion were the only threads to hang on to and Meriel's opinion was never sought. In any case, she was too afraid to speak. Her mother's cold, dark eyes were always on her and the words of duty that the beautiful lips spoke were drummed into her. Duty was a word that she was to hear often.

Within six moths of custody being granted her mother had remarried, her new husband, Francisco Ortiga, a very distant relative on one side of her family, and she had come happily to Venezuela bringing the bright-haired child with her. Even then, Meriel had known that the bitter battle over custody had not been a battle for love of her as far as her mother was concerned. Inez had merely wanted to win.

The marriage was not for love either. Francisco Ortiga wanted another heir, a back-up in case his only son Ramón should either die or be unable to continue the Ortiga line, for there was the inheritance, years of commitment to the name, lands and wealth, and Meriel soon discovered that this was the only source of passion in the luxurious, rambling house.

To Inez, the arrangement was ideal. She was once again in a land where her language was spoken, once again wrapped in the luxury she had left to marry an Englishman, and no emotion was expected of her, only duty.

To Meriel though it was like dying, and her grey eyes had moved from one face to another, from the cool, indifferent face of a stepfather whom she was never to address as anything but *señor*, to the surprised and disgusted faces of the various aunts, uncles and cousins who had travelled many miles to be on hand to greet the new wife and found her half-English daughter's Anglo-Saxon looks and ungainly thinness unacceptable, to the dark, resentful eyes of her new stepbrother.

For Ramón Ortiga had been twenty-two and his resentment had been many-sided. Inez was a usurper who had taken his mother's place too soon and Meriel was an unnecessary oddity thrust into his life with little warning. His attitude had not mellowed either in the months that followed. He knew the reason for the marriage and he looked with displeasure on the fair-haired child who moved like a waif through the house, unable to be dynamic and businesslike, only haltingly speaking the Spanish tongue.

Finally, she had ventured out into the *llanos*, welcoming the wind and the silence, a silence that was peace, so different from the cool and brooding silence of the hacienda. Then she had her first brush with Ramón, for she had wandered a long way when he saw her.

The thunderous drumming of the galloping horse had frightened her badly, but nothing approaching her fear as the horse was reined sharply in and a wildly angry Ramón had slid from the saddle to confront her.

'What do you imagine you are doing here?' His deep voice was harsh, violent, and she had stared at him mesmerised.

'Answer me! What are you doing here?'

'I—I'm going for a walk.'

'A walk!'

To add to her terror he had grasped her long bright hair in one hand, jerking her head upwards as he glared down at her from his intimidating height.

'This is not an English field, you stupid child! This is the *llanos*! Much further and we would have had to turn out the plane to find you—if *el tigre* had not found you first!'

'*El—el tigre?*' She stood uncomfortably in his grasp, her slender neck at an unnatural angle as his hard grip on her hair made movement impossible without further pain.

'*Sí! El tigre!*' He bent his head and glared at her closely. 'The jaguar!' he hissed. 'A big hungry pussycat who would think a little girl a rare delicacy and would not care one little bit that she had shocking bright hair!'

'I can't help my hair!' she had cried, tears beginning to prick her eyes from panic and pain. 'I'm English!'

'You are half Spanish,' he had countered with dark narrowed eyes, but a little burst of misery had prompted her to defy him.

'I don't look it and I don't want to be! I didn't want to come here. I love my father and I don't like the gloomy house and the gloomy people in it!'

For the first time she had seen the black brows raised in aloof astonishment, the wryly twisted lips.

'Including me, English girl?'

'Yes! And I hate you too because you're hurting my head!'

He had released her at once and stepped easily into the saddle, looking down at her as she had taken her courage into both hands and raised her eyes to him.

'So! I am gloomy and you hate me? You will not mind therefore being left here alone to await the coming of *el tigre.* Better to be a pussycat's dinner than to ride with a gloomy savage that you hate, eh?'

'Oh!' Her long-drawn-out gasp and her clenched hands had emphasised the terror in her huge grey eyes and she had seen, also for the first time, the handsome face dissolve into laughter.

With one lithe movement he had bent, his strong arm circling her tiny waist, and she was lifted in front of him to sit high on the great horse as his arm held her securely.

'Perhaps after all I will not leave you to the jaguar,' he mocked, laughter in his voice. 'I will take you home where it is gloomy and filled with gloomy people. You hate them too, *pequeña?*'

'No, I don't hate them. I'm just miserable and they dislike me.' She nestled against him, suddenly warm and secure, and she felt for the first time his hand smooth the wildness of her hair as it blew across his face.

'Do you dislike me, Ramón?' she asked in a very small voice.

'But of course I do! You are after all, English, as you so rightly pointed out.'

There was laughter in his voice and she just knew that he didn't mean it.

For a while she was content to feel the rhythm of the

horse, to look across the peaceful grasslands towards the distant river.

'Is there really a jaguar?' she asked after a while, hopeful that there was not, but all the teasing left his voice and he reined in the horse.

'Can your grey eyes see a long way?' he asked seriously. 'Because if they can you will see the trees that edge the river. Now, in the dry season it is merely a trickle but the roots are deep and they cling to life all the year. In such places *el tigre* hunts for his food and he is a ferocious killer who will attack animals great or small, even if the animal is a man, even if the prey is a bright-haired little girl. *El tigre* is the cat of the *llanos*, seven feet long to the tip of his tail. He can kill with one blow of his paw and he does not always crouch in the trees. Sometimes he ventures further. He will take cattle if he is hungry and he is the enemy of the men who ride the plains. Today you have been foolish. It is better to be unhappy in a gloomy *hacienda* than dead on the open stretches of the *llanos*.'

She shivered and he turned the horse once more for home.

'I—I'll not do it again,' she whispered and he heard her because he asked, 'Is this a promise?'

'Yes.'

'Good. Now I can safely leave you alone at the *hacienda*.'

'Would you care if *el tigre* caught me, Ramón?' she asked tentatively, wanting somebody to care, and he tilted her pale face up, looking down at her with dark arrogant eyes.

'It would have been better if you had not been brought here,' he said evenly, 'but as you are here, then yes, I would care, even though you are English and hate me.'

She smiled up at him with pleasure, her eyes glowing, and for a second he looked straight into the silvery depths, unsmiling, before looking away towards the house. He had said nothing more and when at dinner she had greeted him with a little smile of friendship he had coldly ignored her.

'Dreaming?' His voice dragged her back into the present

and she looked at him with the cool eyes he had so often turned on her.

'Remembering would perhaps be a better word,' she said with no inflection in her voice. 'Re-living memories.'

'And all of them bad?' he asked quietly.

'Yes! Except for Manolito, yes!' She closed her mouth firmly and he did not speak again.

There was a car parked in front of the *hacienda* in a place usually reserved for the cars of visitors and some inner instinct made Meriel stiffen.

'You have another new car?' she asked tautly. 'I thought that you always stuck to Mercedes for a pleasure vehicle.'

'I do.' His voice was as taut as hers and it did nothing to ease her mind. 'The car belongs to Carmen, she has been looking after Manuel.'

'So why am I here as you have all the help that you need?' She swung round in the seat and glared at him, two silvery eyes meeting two dark eyes, an equal amount of anger in both pairs.

'I have told you,' he said sharply, 'Manuel needs you. He has asked for you constantly. At night he wakes up with screams from bad dreams and then he weeps for his sister. Merry! Merry! It is all that we hear and there is no comforting him.'

'As I recall, there is little comfort in Carmen!' she snorted angrily. 'No doubt she is sleeping the sleep of the just while Manolito works himself up into an agony of memories!'

'There is no woman in the house except the servants, what would you have had me do?' he demanded angrily. 'Tia Barbara offered the help of Carmen and I was very grateful!'

Meriel had heard enough and stormed from the car, slamming the door. Yes, Tia Barbara would have offered the help of Carmen. It was the grief of her life that she was aunt to Ramón and her daughter Carmen his first cousin. A marriage between them would have opened the doors for her to the Ortiga wealth but unfortunately the relationship was too close for any marriage to be possible. Nevertheless she insinuated both herself and Carmen into the house on every conceivable occasion and this occasion was an opportunity too good to be missed. Manuel was the last of their worries.

Her burst of rage was stifled as the great doors opened and her half-brother came out into the sunlight. For a moment she stood still, shocked beyond words at the sight of him. There was a deathly pallor beneath the golden tones of his skin and he had lost weight, but some of this she had expected. She had not, however, expected to see a small boy clothed from head to foot in black. His black suit and shoes, his black tie against his stark white shirt looked bizarre and uncomfortable in the heat of the afternoon, and he stood quite still, clearly afraid to come to her, afraid to show any emotion.

'Manolito?' She called to him softly and Ramón, just leaving the car, paused with the same breathless waiting that was on her face.

For a second, the tight face of her half-brother held its blank dignity, and then he flew across the space between them, hurling himself at her, twisting his arms around her waist and burying his face into her.

'Merry! Merry! You have come!'

She could feel his body racked with dry sobs, his hands clutching her tightly in his misery, and the eyes that she turned on the woman who followed Manuel out into the sunlight were harder than her eyes had ever looked in her life. For a moment it seemed that Carmen would speak, would remonstrate with the boy for this unseemly display of emotion, but after one glance into the silvery grey eyes that looked at her with cold anger she thought better of it, summoning up a smile—of sorts.

'You are here at last, Meriel,' she said tightly. 'Welcome to the *hacienda*.'

'Thank you, Carmen, but I need no other welcome than

the one I have just received. I am home!' she stressed the word, a word she would never have used in any other circumstance at this place. 'I am here to look after my brother and I intend to begin right away!'

'I—I will go to my room, Meriel,' Manuel stammered, ashamed now that he had shown such feelings, understanding the silent disapproval on Carmen's face.

'Right! I'll be with you in two shakes!' She was deliberately easy in her speech, modern and casual, and it did not please Carmen. Perhaps it did not please Ramón either because he took her luggage and moved to the house.

'I will speak to you later, Meriel,' he said with an angry quiet, and she nodded distantly. He certainly would but not before she had spoken to him.

'Excuse me.' She brushed past Carmen and entered the cool and silent hall, seeing her suitcases there on the shining, polished boards of the floor, seeing also that Ramón had walked into his study. He glanced at her but continued, leaving the door open in silent invitation although she needed none.

'Why is Manolito dressed from head to foot in black?' she demanded to know, shutting the door firmly behind her as she entered. 'Isn't his misery enough without this ridiculous discomfort?'

'He is obviously in mourning!' he said tightly, turning away.

'And you?' she asked scathingly. 'Are you not in mourning then?' She leaned against the door, folding her arms and watching him coldly.

He looked down at his jeans and checked shirt and then across at the silken green of her dress.

'Apparently not. Neither are you.' She opened her mouth to reply but he cut in sharply before she had the chance. 'For your information, Manuel was not dressed like that when I left to collect you from the airstrip. It is probably Carmen's idea to impress upon you the solemnity of the occasion. You have rarely risen to any occasion, as I recall.'

'There has never been an occasion in this house worth the effort!' she tossed back at him. 'In any case, the past is unimportant. Now that I am here, Carmen can go.'

'You expect me simply to pack her off?' Ramón looked at her with no interest, almost bored. 'Tia Barbara would be offended beyond words.'

'Then offend her!' she advised sharply. 'You ordered me here and now that I have seen Manolito at the mercy of your cousin, wild horses wouldn't drag me away. I intend to look after Manolito and I'll suffer no interference!'

'Restore Manuel to normality and I promise that you will suffer no interference, but remember that I rule the *hacienda*, the land and—the family! I will not countenance any trouble!' He stood facing her, hands in the pockets of his jeans, the black eyes glittering with impatience.

'Normality is an unusual commodity in this house,' she scoffed, returning his stare with an arrogance of her own. 'And what makes you imagine that there will be trouble?' she added with a smile. She was mocking his power, defying him and his gaze became more intent.

'I only have to look at you,' he assured her in a low voice. 'You do not need to do anything at all. You were born to be trouble with your golden hair and silvery eyes. I recognised trouble from the moment that you stepped into the *hacienda* at an age almost equal to Manuel's now.'

'And you were very thankful when I left,' she said woodenly.

He inclined his head in agreement, his smile without humour.

'Well, don't worry,' she said with a forced lightness. 'A few days and I'll be going back to my own life, to my own— kind!' The last phrase came out almost against her will, seeming to fall from her tongue unbidden, and she would have given anything to withdraw it because she saw his eyes flare with a kind of unholy joy.

'You have not forgotten then, Meriel?'

She turned to the door, refusing to answer the silky question.

'Where am I to sleep?'

'Your old room is ready—as it was.'

Startled she turned back, staring into his shuttered face.

'As it was? After almost seven years? My mother told me when she was in London last that the room had been refurnished as an extra guest-room.'

He nodded absently and turned away, beginning to leaf through the papers on his desk.

'She had it changed. I was away at the time. I had it restored to its original state when I returned.'

'Why?' She found her heart fluttering in her throat, a flicker of feeling stirring, and she silenced it at once.

'Why? I do not like changes, as I told you. I will have your suitcases brought up,' he added, coolly dismissing her.

She was glad to go, the dark study intimidated her, reminding her of the number of times she had stood there as a trembling girl while Ramón sat behind the desk berating her. Let him try it now!

She walked along the wide, polished passage to her old room remembering each door, each picture, every small glittering chandelier that lit the dark passages at night. The house was single-storied in the manner of the old *haciendas*, rambling haphazardly as new parts had been added over the years, and she saw it now with adult eyes, noticing its beauty and charm.

Almost opposite her room, the long door of a small, dark closet caught her eye and her heart thumped as she recognised it. Windowless, dark and confining, it had terrified her as a child.

She walked towards it and pulled open the door, facing her ghosts with tight lips and then stopping in astonishment. It was painted white inside now and filled with shelves that held beautiful bed linen. A light came on automatically as the door opened and her ghost vanished as if it had never been. If Ramón did not like change, he had certainly made an exception here, had wiped out a part of her past that still haunted her mind, a day when Ramón had made it clear that he would one day rule the Ortigas, a day when he had firmly taken her under his protection and destroyed her mother's domination forever.

She walked in a kind of daze to her room, her mind only vaguely noting that it was truly as it had been. Even her small treasures had been brought back from the store room and replaced exactly in the original positions. Rosita! Meriel smiled, fingering the small objects that belonged to the past. Rosita, the small and round housekeeper, had always been fond of her. She wandered to the window and looked across the green of the lawns but her mind was still outside the room, seeing the past and her trial by terror.

It had been a few weeks after her encounter with Ramón on the dry hot plains that she had had the temerity to answer back when her mother had sharply rebuked her for some small fall from grace. Her tiny defiance had brought a punishment that her father had never allowed. She had been locked in the cupboard.

At first as her mother turned the key, leaving her in darkness, she had clung to her defiance, standing against the wall, waiting for her eyes to grow accustomed to the darkness, trying not to hear the steady tapping of her mother's high heels as she walked away. But the blackness was total, confining and suffocating and she had begun to cry, at first softly but then with deep shuddering sobs that threatened to choke her. She had felt for the door and hammered on it in growing panic, knowing that no one would come until her hour of imprisonment was over—her mother had assured her of that.

She began to scream, falling to her knees by the door, surrounded by darkness, and a slowly creeping silence that only her own cries of terror kept at bay, but no one would come.

Ramón had come. She had never heard the sound of his

riding-boots striding along the passage, had heard nothing of his savage voice. Only the feel of his arms as he lifted her, tear-drenched and dirty-faced, to hold her against his chest, awoke her to the fact that she was free.

He had stormed back to the *sala*, his pitiful burden cradled against his shirt, murderous rage in his dark eyes, and he had burst in upon his father and stepmother as they had sat calmly taking tea.

What he had said she never knew, she was not then fluent in Spanish and could not follow the savage speed, but her mother had paled at his obvious threats and his father too had fallen silent before such rage. She was never punished again by her mother; her only ordeal thereafter had been the sharp edge of Ramón's tongue.

It had dawned on her that he had only just come in because his horse was still standing saddled against the stables and he had mounted, grim-faced, pulling her against his chest and riding out on to the *llanos*.

It was a wild ride, the horse at full gallop, the tall grasses parting before the pounding hooves. Her hair had streamed out over his shoulder and gradually her shuddering had stopped as the wind blew in her face and the sun warmed her fear-chilled skin.

When he reined the horse to a stop they were all breathless, Meriel, the horse and Ramón.

'You are free, little one,' he had told her quietly, 'free on the *llanos*, under the sky, the wind in your hair.'

'Why did you leave me so long?'

She had turned her head and timidly touched him as he looked down at her tear-stained face.

'I was not there. Rosita told me as I came in. It will not happen again.'

Gently he had removed her hand, looking for a moment at her thin, pale fingers, and then he had turned for home, silent and stern, but a haven of comfort and protection. Not that it had made her very much more happy, only perhaps a little more secure, for he had continued in the same manner as before, cold and aloof, ignoring her, speaking to her only when she spoke to him, and she had no doubt whatever that she was an outsider.

What it had done however was give her mother the excuse that she needed to send her away. Her father had applied once more for custody, complaining that with Meriel in Venzuela his visiting rights were an impossibility, and for once, Inez had been prepared to compromise. Her tutor had been dismissed and Meriel had been packed off to boarding school in England only to come out to the *hacienda* in the long holidays and at Christmas. Her father could visit her as often as he wished and she could spend the short holidays with him. Inez had rid herself of the ignominy of Ramón dictating to her about her conduct with her own child, and Meriel was not a constant reminder of her English marriage.

Ramón had put her on the plane and she had seen a kind of satisfaction in his dark eyes too.

José brought up her suitcases and greeted her with his old face wreathed in smiles. She was not surprised to find that Ramón had handed them over to a servant, he would not wish to see more of her than was necessary, and she quickly hung up her clothes and put a fresh skirt and top on the bed, ready to change and then seek out Manuel.

She was surprised therefore to hear a sharp knock on the door and find Ramón outside as she opened it.

'You have everything that you need?' He stood looking down at her with eyes that were oddly intent and for a second she simply looked back, not answering. 'It is strange to find you once again in the house,' he added quietly. 'It is something that we will both have to get used to.'

'I shall be here for only a little while,' she said tightly, turning away and walking into her room. 'I'm quite sure that with Carmen out of the way and Manolito free to talk or weep as he wishes my job here will soon be over. In any case,' she added, 'I can't take indefinite leave. My leave is open-ended only because I ...' She suddenly pulled up short. Her relationship with Stewart was nothing to do with Ramón Ortiga.

'Only because you are on very close terms with the owner of the Mackensie Press,' he finished for her, leaning against the door and apparently settling in for a good while.

'How do you know anything about me?' she asked sharply, her face colouring at the smile of amusement on his dark face.

'You have seen Inez and Manuel quite often during the past three years,' he reminded her. 'Certainly they have made plenty of visits to England. I did not particularly like your mother but I did hold conversations with her in the normal course of a day. She was very proud of your success and never failed to talk of your work at great length.'

'I'm sorry,' she rejoined tartly. 'You must have been unspeakably bored.'

'Not at all,' he countered easily. 'It is only natural that I would be interested in the welfare of my stepsister, surely? Have I not always been interested in your welfare?'

'Only in a very vague way,' she said shooting him a bitter glance. 'Only when you had the chance to criticise me and take me to task,' she added unfairly.

'You were somewhat of a trial,' he murmured, his eyes moving over her with a curious intensity. 'I feel that perhaps you will still be a trial.' He turned to leave and then glanced at her over his shoulder. 'You left the door open when you went to explore your—cupboard. I have closed it. Does this come under the heading of criticism?'

Meriel stared at the blank face of her bedroom door as he closed it. He had given her a timely reminder of the way he had cared for her and she felt suddenly distraught. She showered and dressed angrily, fighting down the feelings of guilt. He had protected her in his aloof and half-amused way, so what? She had been a child and his domination

over her had been partly so that he could show her mother
that she might be the new wife of Francisco Ortiga but she
was in no way in charge of anything, not even her own
daughter. He had never been kind to her. She bit her lip
and shook her head. Yes, he had. Honesty made her admit
it. In his own way he had been more than kind, there had
been a sort of love between the clever, hard-riding, deep-
thinking man and the lonely child she had been. What did
she owe him? Nothing! He had finally wiped out the
intervening years with his callous rejection of her, and had
it not been for her altered relationship with her mother, she
would never have been able to keep in touch with
Manolito.

Even now, she was not sure what had finally drawn her
mother to England over the past three years. They had
written to each other of course, dutiful letters that had said
nothing, but suddenly, Inez had arrived and there was a
difference in her, a desire to work out some sort of
relationship with a daughter she had treated with
indifference for all her young life. Perhaps it was the
staggering isolation of the *hacienda* or the fact that she was
able to see Manolito growing away from his sister. Meriel
had not really cared. It was not in her to continue her life
with bitterness. Her job was satisfying, her life exciting and
she had welcomed her mother and Manolito with a great
deal of happiness, glad that Inez had been more than
willing to meet her half-way in her attempts to set things
right at last. Her love for Manolito had never faded and
now, in her own familiar background, she had been able to
show him how she cared, her happiness rubbing off on him
until they were back into the way they had always been.

Now, she had nothing but the memories, but at least they
were happy ones, going some way to ease the burden of her
stay here and the bad memories that were rooted in this
house. Clearly, Ramón would never have allowed her to see
her brother and though he had called her back so
imperiously, she was not deceived. He wanted help,

temporary help, until Manolita had recovered from the shock of losing his parents.

She dressed and went to find him, determined that he should not be left to be lonely and lost as she had been, secretly determined too that if the chance came her way, she would get him out of here and back to England. He could live with her, go to an English school, be free of the *llanos* and Ramón, free from the responsibility of the Ortiga line and the Ortiga inheritance.

CHAPTER THREE

MERIEL stayed with Manuel until dinner time, talking to him and walking with him in the gardens. She had persuaded him out of the black suit and tie into jeans and a soft shirt and this had not gone unnoticed by Carmen, but she said nothing to either of them.

She had spoken to Ramón, however, because he called Meriel to his study as she made her way along in good time for dinner, still in the thin flowered skirt and cream blouse that she had donned earlier.

'Carmen is angry and hurt,' he began without preamble as he closed the study door behind her.

'I'm startled and grieved,' Meriel said dramatically, opening her eyes wide in mock alarm and apparently angering him too.

'Could you not have waited for her to go before you began to throw your weight about?' he rasped. 'What difference would a couple of days more have meant!'

'All the difference in the world!' she snapped, not amused any more. 'She may as well know who is in charge right from the word go.'

'I am in charge,' Ramón reminded her dangerously. 'Also the word go will come from me—when I wish her to leave. In the meantime I would be greatly obliged if you could keep a modicum of civility in your tongue and a little courtesy in your behaviour.'

'You,' she said, her voice rising, 'demanded my return to the *hacienda*. According to your telephone call and the things you have said since, Manolito needed me. She is complaining, I suppose, that I have persuaded him to remove the black clothes, wash his face and relax into being a boy, a child. I suppose that at some time in your life you were a child? Or don't you remember?'

38

'I remember,' he said harshly. 'I was tossed into the saddle at five and was bidden to ride. I was lectured on my responsibilities and charged with the security of my inheritance. At fourteen I was expected to be able to ride a full day with the men and spend the evening with my father on the matter of the family business interests. I remember! Manuel is not expected to do any of these things, the responsibility is mine and I will not have the house turned upside down because of your inability to keep a civilised tongue in your head and your English opinion of what is correct and incorrect!'

'What part of my English character were you expecting to be of use to Manolito when you ordered me home then?' she enquired, keeping her voice sharp to disguise the sudden tilting of her heart at the bitter picture he painted.

'Once,' he said more quietly, 'you had a gentleness, a gentleness that was very alien in this family. If anyone brought out the best in me then it was you. It is your gentleness that Manuel needs now, if you still indeed possess it. I think that somewhere you must possess it because although I have not seen you for so long, Manuel has seen you and pined for you. You even managed to mellow your mother in her later years. Give Manuel your love. I will fight for him and it would be better too if you and I did not fight each other because odd though it may seem to you, Manuel is fond of me and will be further torn apart at any sign of discord between you and me.'

She looked at him for a moment and then turned away, chastened. There was no fight left in her and she remembered only too well that he was always scrupulously fair.

'All right, I'm sorry.' She suddenly gave a light laugh as she reached for the door. 'It's funny, that's twice that I've offered my apologies. I suppose that I've become very much accustomed to doing whatever I like and to having people bow and scrape a little. You certainly bring me down to earth and make me realise that in the content of the wide,

wide world I'm very small fry, not nearly as important as I sometimes feel.'

She felt his hands on her shoulders as she reached the door and he turned her towards him.

'Yes, Miss Curtis. Your call from Venezuela, Miss Curtis,' he mocked softly. She suddenly found herself laughing with genuine amusement looking into smiling mocking eyes.

'All right. So you heard my working image. I take your point—all your points.' He said nothing but continued to look down into her face and she found the smile dying on her lips as they simply became lost in each other's eyes.

'Meriel,' he said in little more than a murmur, his voice fading away altogether as he let his gaze roam over her face, and she did not resist when he drew her closer, close enough for her to feel the heavy beating of his heart.

'I—I must go to dinner . . . Manolito is coming now . . .' Her voice too died away and her breath was thick in her throat at the taut, harsh expression on his face. 'Ramón! No!'

He ignored her, drawing her tightly against him and swooping down to cover her lips with his, his hands tight on her back, his mouth harsh and plundering. He had clearly known that she would fight and therefore he attacked, leaving her no room for manoeuvre until she sighed, a mere whisper of sound, and rested against him.

She had always reacted to Ramón. Even as a child she had needed his approval above all others and later . . . She stiffened, memory coming to her aid, and he was ready for that too, drawing back and trailing one lazy finger-tip down her face.

'Why—why did you do that?' She struggled like someone fighting her way out of a deep dream, her body still and drugged but her mind clamouring frantically.

'I wanted to see if you remembered.' His dark eyes bored into hers holding her gaze with such ease. 'You do remember.'

He was laughing at her, she could see it at the back of his

narrowed eyes and it snapped her into reality and anger.

'Don't ever do that again!' she blazed, her temper and humiliation at her response to him flaring.

'If that is an order then I do not obey orders, I give them,' he told her softly. 'If, on the other hand, you require a promise then you know that I keep my promises and I am not about to make a promise that I cannot keep,' he reached forward and ran the back of his fingers across her hot cheeks, 'that I may not wish to keep.'

'If you try your amorous tactics on me again—I'll leave!' she threatened heatedly, springing away like someone burned. 'You were never short of women as I recall. It's perhaps time that you had a new one!'

'There have been plenty,' he agreed, laughing into her flushed face. 'Many since you left the *hacienda*, so young and sweet. You would have me be an innocent boy—inexperienced, gauche?'

'I wouldn't have you gift-wrapped!' she snapped, flinging the door open. 'And don't forget, next time, I leave!'

'If I let you,' he warned in a low taunting voice. 'It is a very long way to England.'

She didn't deign to answer and it took all her efforts to be even reasonably civilised at dinner, especially when Carmen felt the need to point out quietly but sourly the unsuitability of the casual clothes that Manuel wore, her eyes including Meriel for good measure.

'I expect he is comfortable,' Ramón cut in before Meriel could explode. 'Which brings me to a point. Tomorrow I am flying to Caracas on business, I am meeting one of the engineers from the mine. I shall take Meriel and Manuel with me. I understand from Manuel that his sister is not satisfied with the state of his wardrobe. Obviously he needs more clothes and it will be a good time for her to get them. The plane will easily take four and your luggage, Carmen. You can come with us and then fly on down the coast to your home.'

Meriel did not know who was the more surpised, Carmen

or herself, certainly they were both silenced, and from the corner of her eye she saw her brother trying hard to disguise his relief.

'Well, if you can manage without me . . .'

'We can.' Ramón smiled warmly at his cousin. 'You have been a treasure but I know that Tia Barbara will be missing you, she is no longer young.'

'No.' Pride, duty and disappointment warred in her face. 'I suppose you are right, Ramón. I must confess too that it is a little lonely here on the plains.'

'You have been very brave,' Ramón soothed, his eyes perfectly serious.

'Well—I, well thank you.' Carmen preened but could not resist a final shot at Meriel. 'I do hope that you will not be too lonely here, Meriel. It's not London after all and I do remember your loneliness and unhappiness when you were here as as child—and even later.'

'Yes, I was unhappy,' Meriel agreed. 'I have never after all been part of the life of the Ortigas and naturally I wouldn't want to be, being more English than Spanish. However I do have a job after all, it's not that I'll be here permanently. I expect that my boss will be demanding my return before too long. We have a very close working relationship.'

'Meriel will be too busy to become lonely,' Ramón growled impatiently, 'and her leave will be extended as far as is necessary!'

'I do hope that you're right,' Meriel intervened sweetly. 'Stewart is so used to my being there every time he wants me. He really has taken this badly.'

Whether Carmen's tight lips denoted that she thought having a job an undignified way of managing one's life or whether she had caught the veiled innuendoes in Meriel's remarks, Meriel was not sure. She knew though that Ramón had caught every innuendo and his black scowl was proof of it. He turned to speak to his cousin, cutting Meriel out with practised ease, he had done that to her all her life and when the two were in deep conversation, Manuel tugged at her sleeve.

'Merry? You will not leave me?' His dark anxious eyes, so endearingly like Ramón's, looked up into hers and she secretly squeezed his hand.

'Never in a million years,' she whispered. 'Sometimes I tell the most awful lies just to see what people will do.'

He giggled, stifling his merriment quickly as Ramón looked coldly across and Meriel raised innocent grey eyes as he shot her a look of narrow-eyed suspicion and annoyance. It was nothing new. She stared at him, trying to summon up dislike and annoyance, but she was unable to do either. Although he talked only to Carmen for the rest of the meal, his eyes were solely on Meriel and she was glad when the ordeal was over and she was once again in her own room, Manuel tucked safely up in bed showing some signs of relaxation and happiness.

There was no happiness in her though, and for a long time she tossed restlessly beneath the silken sheets. The day had seemed endless and she had found cracks in her armour as far as Ramón was concerned. He was already slipping out of his niche as cold stepbrother into something much more potent in her mind. She had been here before in this situation but then she had been defenceless, a girl, she needed all the years away to help her to stay free in her heart.

Memories came flooding back in the darkness, memories she could not hold away even though she tried. Life here had been difficult enough, her holidays in Venezuela a duty that must be endured, and only the rides with Ramón, his strength and protection, gave her any kind of confidence, although he had little time for her, his attention to her sandwiched between his own duties and work and the women who frequently came to the *hacienda* as his guests.

It had taken four years to change the relationship between them, and for her it had changed subtly and frighteningly. She was growing and more than ever unsure of herself, neither child nor woman. She only knew that

Ramón stayed in her mind more than he had ever done and the sight of him as she landed for the long summer holidays gave a queer lift to her heart, the cool kiss he invariably placed on her cheek the reward she waited for during the long months away. She would not have wanted to leave her father but the excitement that the thought of meeting Ramón brought was like a fire growing inside her.

She was taller then at sixteen than she had promised to be as a child, already filling out into the slender, softly rounded shape of a woman, but basically there was no change in her life at all. She arrived, was coolly greeted, rode with Ramón when he was not too busy, but her place at the *hacienda* of the Ortigas was set and firm, she was an outsider and she never felt more so than when the beautiful women that Ramón knew came to stay. Then, she saw nothing of him, and any intrusion on her part was deeply frowned upon by her handsome stepbrother. At these times, she longed for the holidays to end but shed many bitter tears when they did, always in secret, always in complete control of herself when Ramón drove her back to the airstrip.

The Christmas holiday when she had been sixteen and a half stood out miserably in her mind. The house had been full of guests, the Ortigas of course in full force, all of them ignoring her with the exception of one distant cousin of Ramón whose attentions were an embarrassment, especially as it drew Ramón's disapproving eyes in her direction. He only seemed to notice her when Ricard Ortiga was there, and then he glared at her with a message that told her so obviously that she was stepping out of her place even to think of encouraging such attention.

She had wandered out into the courtyard and across to the stables and from there, drawn by the music coming from the quarters of the *llaneros*, she had lingered to watch them celebrating the fiesta in their own way, her own miseries partly forgotten as she watched them dance and listened to the guitars until she forgot the length of time she had been there.

Ramón's harsh voice had reminded her, his hand on her arm strong and impelling.

'What are you doing here?' he had demanded to know as he came behind her, swinging her round to face his hard and angry eyes.

'I—I'm watching the *llaneros*,' she stammered, wildly searching in her mind as to any crime she might have committed without knowing it. 'I love to see them dance the *joropo* and see them all dressed up like this in white.'

'They are not on display for the curious!' he bit out harshly. 'This is a holiday for them and God knows they get few days out of the saddle. They can well do without any interested bystanders. Leave them alone! If you are seeking admiring male attention then you will have to make do with Ricard!'

He had been forcibly leading her away as he spoke and now she stopped, gazing up at him with shocked and hurt surprise, tears beginning to well up inside at his cruel tones and his unjust accusations. Many times before she had watched the men dancing, even joining in as their womenfolk had shown her the steps. They were her friends in their quiet and polite way and she understood their hard but kindly faces, knew the harsh life they lived. He had never objected before and she could not understand this sudden and violent attack.

She pulled away and ran into the garden, seeking the shelter of an arbour that had been her refuge many times when she was unhappy, sinking to the garden seat and crying quietly and bitterly, lost in her own misery and utterly alone.

'I am not supposed to see you cry, am I?' Ramón's deep voice startled her. She had supposed that, his mission completed, he would have gone back to his guests, to the glittering ladies who flocked around him. She turned away, her head bent, moving along the seat from him when he sat beside her. 'Many times nowadays you cry, do you not, Meriel?' he asked quietly. 'Never though, with me, never so that I may ask why you weep. Always it is in secret, your tears dried, your face composed before you meet me again.'

'I—I don't,' she managed, fighting to control her tears and the bitter hurt. 'You've annoyed me, that's all. You've annoyed me because it's not fair. I often cry when I'm really angry and you know full well that I've been going to see the *llaneros* since I was a little girl. I often speak to them when we're riding together. I speak to their wives too. I have been doing so ever since my Spanish became fluent.'

'I do know this—full well, as you say,' he assured her deeply. 'Also do not lie to me, you are not very good at it. You are hurt, not angry. You will have to realise that you are not now a child who can come and go at will. The *llaneros* are men, not all of them married, and you are growing up to be a very beautiful girl, almost a woman.'

'I am?' She turned tear-drenched eyes on him and his harsh face softened.

'Do you not know it?' he asked in little more than a whisper of sound. 'There are ladies up at the *hacienda* who are in no doubt of your growing beauty and maturity. They know very well too that they are women. One day you will know it and that will be a day to remember.'

'I don't understand you, Ramón,' she said tremulously, an unexpected shiver running over her as he moved closer along the seat.

'Perhaps you are not meant to understand me,' he said softly, 'or perhaps it is because you are still struggling out of your childhood and into a new kind of beauty. Half-way between the two, you are enchanting—and very vulnerable,' he added seriously. 'Do not wander alone among men who have eyes in their heads that see your beauty and vulnerability. Ricard is enough to cope with at the moment. If I have to break a nose, I would prefer to break his. The men are important to me, he is not.'

She stared at him with wide and troubled eyes, her face losing its pale sheen and glowing with soft colour.

'Is that why—why you glared at me when—when . . . I thought you were angry with me for being friendly to him because he's an Ortiga.'

'*Por Diós!*' For a moment, black anger crossed his face, but he controlled it at her quick look of alarm, his hand coming to her hair, running the tresses through his fingers, watching the golden strands fall to her shoulders.

'I think that it will be a long time before you are really able to take care of yourself, *pequeña*,' he said quietly. 'Even your thoughts run on lines that are utterly innocent and sweet.' He stood abruptly and pulled her to her feet.

'Come, you wish to dance? Put on that dress that I saw you trying on in front of the mirror as I passed your room last night, the long white one. Soon there will be dancing at the *hacienda* and I will dance with you. So far I have taught you everything else, I may as well continue with the lessons.'

'I can dance,' she said with a shy little smile,' we often go to dances from school.'

'With boys?' he enquired with mocking amazement, his hand coming to her chin as she blushed and would have hidden her face.

'Yes,' she said with a touch of defiance. 'Naturally there are boys.'

'And do they also tell you that you are beautiful?' he enquired softly, tilting her face to his, his eyes intently on her soft blushes.

'N-no, we're all just—just friends.'

'Ah! Then they are still only boys,' he said with a softly mocking smile. 'One day there will be someone who is not a boy. Before that day comes I will have to write to this English school and inform the one in charge that my stepsister is not to be allowed out without an escort of two ugly teachers.'

'Oh! Ramón, you wouldn't!' She gasped, completely taken in by his serious face, but his soft laughter stopped her sudden anxiety and he took her hand, drawing her along with him and back to the house.

'I am not sure yet exactly what I will do,' he confessed quietly. 'You will have to wait and see.'

'Please, Ramón,' she said with renewed anxiety, 'I don't

want you to interfere with school. I'm quite safe and I hate having attention drawn to me. It's bad enough as it is.'

'What is bad enough, little one?' he asked seriously, stopping and looking down at her, his keen gaze making her blush anew.

'Just—just . . . things,' she murmured, dropping her gaze.

'Then I will not make—things worse,' he promised softly. 'We will just dance and you can show me how well you do that. It will also serve to get Ricard out of your hair and into his proper place.'

'What place is that?' she asked with sudden mischief and he lifted her hand, surprising her by kissing it gently.

'No place at all,' he assured her quietly, 'not because he is an Ortiga but because you are—Meriel. He is way down the line. Come.'

If his words had puzzled her and confused her, his actions later left her utterly bewildered. She changed into the white dress. It was a dreamy dress, she thought, as she stood and looked at herself. There were layers of chiffon, the sleeves puffed and demure, the neckline round and simple, and her golden hair shone in the lights as she went to the *sala*, drawn by the sound of the music. She hesitated outside, feeling unsure, and suddenly again unwelcome, but before she could retreat the door opened and Ramón stood there in dark suit, his black hair glittering in the light, and he caught her hand.

'Aha!' he said in mocking triumph. 'Caught you! You were about to flee, being once again quite sure that you are without value.'

'I—I was going to . . .'

'Run away!' he finished firmly. 'Come, we will dance. Hide your fears. Remember who you are.'

'I don't know who I am,' she said sadly and softly as he led her into the well lit room where every eye seemed to turn on them, her nervous shiver bringing Ramón's arms round her as he swept her into the rhythm of the dance without any preamble.

'A delightful amnesia that will one day totally disap-

pear,' he assured her. 'For now, you look quite beautiful
and fresh as a morning rose. Ricard on the other hand looks
a pale shade of green. I never noticed before how ugly he is.
Strange!'

Meriel giggled and he looked down at her with a smile,
his hands tightening on her waist.

'You will avoid him, *pequeña*?' he asked quietly and she
nodded happily, blissfully secure in his strong arms, her
happiness spilling over when he complimented her on her
dancing and on the white dress that was so commonplace
beside the gowns of the other women there.

'The others have really beautiful dresses,' she reminded
him, a little embarrassed when his eyes went with open
speculation over the ladies in question, his gaze lingering
on their bare shoulders and the necklines that seemed to her
to be little short of shocking.

'You wish to look like that?' he enquired, his gaze
coming back to hers, and she shook her head, hiding behind
thick lashes to avoid his intent eyes. 'I am glad that you do
not, otherwise, I would not only write to the school, I would
come and personally supervise your wardrobe.'

'You—you know I wouldn't . . .' she began, worried at
his burst of anger, and he suddenly laughed, pulling her to
him and swirling her around faster.

'You are very anxious to keep me away from England,'
he said mockingly.

'You are afraid that my bullying will follow you to your
own world?'

'No! You don't bully me, well, not often, and then you're
almost always right. I'm not trying to keep you away from
England either, I often wish you were there,' she added
daringly.

'Why?' he asked with quiet but determined force.

'Sometimes—sometimes, I—I miss you,' she said softly,
hanging her head to avoid his keen, dark eyes.

'It is only natural,' he said quietly. 'I am your stepbrother
after all, and I have had a great deal to do with your life in
the past.'

He said nothing more and she wondered rather

miserably if her confession had annoyed him, but it seemed that it had not because he held her with a gentleness that was beautiful, and his voice was soft in her ear.

'Do not worry,' he urged quietly. 'One day you will be safe to let out alone.'

'You mean that I'll grow into a big girl?' she asked with a sudden waspish anger and he drew back to look at her.

'We must hope not,' he said seriously even though his dark eyes shone with laughter. 'You are now—almost perfect.' His flashing gaze skimmed over her slender shape and she blushed deeply, wishing she had held her tongue, her trembling not stopping for a long while as he danced with her for the better part of the evening to the clear annoyance of the ladies present and the open disgust of Ricard. It was the most wonderful night of her life but her happiness did not last. The next day she was relegated to her place, Ramón ignored her again and things were back to normal, but she kept well away from his cousin and she was glad to see them all leave, even though it meant that Ramón was now out on the *llanos* from morning until night.

She was not protected from the Ortigas though, nor was she freed from the added unhappiness that they brought into her life. A change in the pattern of the school holidays due to the refurbishing of the school building made her next birthday fall when she was actually at the *hacienda*. Before, she had been taken out to dinner by her father, had received small gifts from her friends at school and a large expensive one from her mother, never anything from Ramón to show that he remembered whether she was alive or dead, so she dreaded her next birthday, her seventeenth.

She came to the breakfast table on the day in a very uneasy state of mind, already hot with imagined embarrassment because she was sure that no one would remember and she would rather that they did not remember later and know of her disappointment. There were gifts though, arranged round her plate by Rosita, and her mother had made the effort to be early to greet her, Manuel bubbling with excitement at her side.

There was a silver bracelet from her father, a parcel from

school with the usual amusing gifts that made her laugh, a beautiful Indian cloak from her mother and a small musical box from the five-year-old Manuel.

'Mama and I bought it in Caracas a long time ago,' he confided proudly. 'I have kept it wrapped in my drawer and never taken it out,' he shot her a dark, anxious glance, 'well, not very often.'

'Oh, darling, it's beautiful!' She bent to hug him and her eyes met Ramón's as he stood leaning against the door. He said nothing, not even wishing her a happy birthday, and her eyes hid from him in distress. She had not expected a gift from her stepfather, she often thought that Francisco Ortiga failed to realise who she was, his eyes only fell on her in a vague surprise, but Ramón was different and he had not even greeted her.

She threw herself into the mood of Manuel, sitting him on her knee and letting him open the small presents from school, laughing with him at the amusing things that were all her friends ever gave to each other, trying to forget that Ramón was still there.

He waited until Manuel had jumped down to the floor and then he moved, bringing from behind his back a perfectly arranged spray of yellow roses, walking across the room and placing them in her hands.

'Many happy returns. This is what they say in England?'

'Yes, they're beautiful. Thank you, Ramón.'

He stared down into her eyes for a long time until her face grew hot and then he smiled, a long, slow smile.

'They are a greeting only. They are not your gift because it cannot be brought to the table and placed around your plate. Come.'

He took her hand gently, pulling her to her feet, motioning the excited Manuel away with a severe look that warned him not to follow, and Meriel walked beside him from the room, her hand securely held, her heart pounding wildly.

Ramón led her to the back of the house, urging her on when she hesitated, his face quite serious as they came to the cobbled yard by the stables. There was a foal there, large eyed and timid, its coat as black as jet, shining in the early sunlight.

'Your gift.' He pointed at the foal and let her go but she had been frozen to the spot, stunned with disbelief.

'For me?' She turned to him, her grey eyes as big and wide as the foal's, and he laughed then, taking her hand again and urging her towards the beautiful creature.

'I could not resist it. It reminded me of you, long-legged and timid, gentle and beautiful. Unfortunately, he is black, there are no yellow horses although I looked for a whole year.'

They walked to the foal and she touched it lovingly and shyly and then in a burst of affection and gratitude she turned and threw her arms around Ramón's waist, hugging him tightly, forgetting his aloof manner.

'Oh, Ramón! Thank you, thank you!'

For a brief second, he stiffened and her heart lurched with worry that she had stepped beyond the bounds allowed, showing an emotion that was unacceptable, and then his arms tightened round her, holding her close in the quiet and sunny courtyard, silence all around them. A new fear leapt into her throat when he gently tilted her chin, looking down into her wide and anxious eyes, his own eyes dark and glittering.

'I—I'm sorry,' she whispered. 'I'm behaving like an idiot.' She made to move away from the warm and enfolding arms but he held her closely still, his eyes on the softness of her lips as she gazed up into his eyes.

'You are not alone in that,' he said softly. 'There is an idiot in both of us, waiting to get out.' He seemed to be hypnotised by her mouth and by the soft flush of colour that flared in her cheeks and slowly his head bent to hers until he was almost touching her lips with his, his breath warm on her face.

'I have to be very careful how I treat you,' he murmured in an old voice, speaking as though his mind was on something else entirely. 'You are very—breakable.' An overwhelming desire to close her eyes had her dark lashes falling slowly so that when his lips finally touched her, she was in an odd and trance-like state, her breathing slow and shallow.

His lips came to the delicate corner of her mouth, lingering there for a second and then lifting to move to the other side and gently rest there. Then, suddenly, he laughed and put her gently away. 'I will turn him into the paddock and we will see him run,' he said with no emotion in his voice. 'He must be trained. While you are in England I will school him when he is old enough and one day we will see how you ride a thoroughbred horse across the *llanos*.'

'If I'm here,' she said softly, leaning against the fence and watching the foal kick his heels and race in circles of pleasure on the grass. 'I'm seventeen today. When I am eighteen I shall be leaving school and then I'll not be coming back.'

'What do you mean?' He had turned on her harshly as if she had been deliberately defying him. 'This is your home!'

'Not really.' She looked up at him and then looked away from the dark anger of his eyes, mournful that she had angered him but knowing that he would probe until he had the truth. 'I can do whatever I wish when I'm eighteen and I've decided not to go to university. I want to go straight into a job and my father knows the owner of a big chain of magazines. He's an old man but my father went to school with his son. The son is dead now but they've always kept up correspondence and when I told my father what I'd decided he got me an interview with Mr Mackensie. I can start with them when I go back to England after the next summer holiday. I'm going into advertising, selling it.'

'You!' Ramón burst into laughter, his hands coming to span her slim waist. 'You are too shy to ask for more tea when you are at the table! How do you expect to sell advertising? This type of work is very hard and competitive.'

'I know.' She was hurt by his laughter and her lips trembled. 'I'll have to get hard and businesslike. I'll have to be more like the Ortigas,' she finished defiantly.

'But I like you as you are,' he had said softly, tightening his grip on her. 'I like to have a shy and gentle stepsister who watches me with wide and anxious eyes. I do not want a modern impressive salesperson striding around the *hacienda* telling me how to manage my affairs.'

He had to be joking, although he looked perfectly serious and she smiled tentatively, unsure.

'But you forget what I said, Ramón!' she said softly. 'I will not be coming here. I shall be working in England and the times when I can visit will be very few.' He stared down at her and then suddenly lifted her by the waist, holding her above him and glaring up into her face. She could see that he was angry enough to throw her over the fence and into the field and she couldn't even reach to touch his shoulders, he had her too high up.

'You will beg my pardon and refuse this ridiculous job!' he rapped out, his dark eyes blazing.

'I have to earn my living,' she stammered in a frightened voice.

'Promise!' He held her even higher and she nodded frantically until he lowered her to the ground, continuing to look furious.

'Let us have no more of these ridiculous ideas,' he ground out, taking her shoulder and turning her towards the house, 'you will live here at the *hacienda* when you have finished at school!'

'I can't! I—I can't, Ramón!' She had to continue even though she was frightened by his anger. 'If I live here permanently, I'll never see my father!'

He stopped for a second and looked down at her as if the thought was entirely new to him but then turned her back towards the gardens and the house.

'He will visit you here.' Apparently that was to be the end of it.

'How can he? He's not rich like you. He could hardly ever come.'

'Then you will visit him and I will pay for it. Do be quiet

now, I have heard enough!'

Her trembling legs stumbled and she would have fallen headlong but his arm shot out and caught her.

'Ah! You are so afraid that your legs will not walk. Remember that the next time you have such wildly irritating ideas.'

'They're not . . .!' she began but his arm tightened and he drew her close in a comforting embrace.

'Always there has been this small seed of defiance in you,' he murmured. 'Let us hope that it does not grow and blossom or you and I will clash badly.'

His free hand stroked her neck as he looked down at her, his thumb moving in a sort of hard caress along her jawline, and suddenly his embrace was not comforting any more. A frightening excitement raced along her nerve-endings and she lowered her lashes nervously.

Colour flooded her face, making her grey eyes wild and shining as she glanced timidly up at him again and he smiled, his long, slow smile.

'Beautiful!' he said softly. 'Almost perfect. You have only one flaw.' He paused and she searched his face with anxious eyes, waiting with her breath shallow and uneven as he added with deliberate mockery, 'You are English.'

'That's not a flaw,' she whispered, feeling oddly faint and shaky.

'Perhaps it is a flaw to me,' he said softly, leading her to the house, his arm still around her.

She had raised her eyes to see the anger and shock on the face of Doña Barbara who stood in the doorway flanked by a disapproving Carmen and a brilliantly beautiful woman she had never seen before. Ramón's aunt looked like a Captain of the Guard with an escort of two troopers and she bristled with an annoyance barely held in check at the sight of Ramón's arm around his stepsister.

'You have arrived early, Tia Barbara,' Ramón observed, clearly surprised to see her at all.

'We stayed overnight at Caracas and left at first light,' his aunt replied, making a very great effort at charm and not quite succeeding. 'I phoned ahead for the car but clearly you did not get my message. Fortunately someone did because that rogue Silva met us at the airstrip and here we are.'

And just in time apparently, her tone said, as she looked with ill-concealed dislike at Meriel.

'It is Meriel's birthday,' Ramón said off-handedly. 'I have bought her a black foal. We have been viewing it.'

His eyes were on the woman beside his aunt and his obvious interest banished the disapproval from Doña Barbara's face.

'I have brought Señorita Sandoval to stay with us over the weekend. Her family are old friends. I'm sure you have heard of her father, Ramón? He is in mining.'

'Ah yes, we have met, but I did not realise that he had such a charming daughter. Your servant, Señorita Sandoval.'

He bowed, graciously, charmingly, all too clearly interested, and Meriel walked quickly to the house, gathering her gifts and taking Manuel's hand. They were leaving as Ramón brought his visitors back into the *hacienda*.

'How lovely to see such affection between the children,' Doña Barbara observed in a sweetly poisonous voice. 'Obviously there is a great fondness, even though they are so oddly unalike.'

'But you forget, Tia Barbara,' Ramón said mockingly, his eyes on Meriel's flushed face, 'Meriel is English— proudly English. She is not like us at all.'

It had hurt badly and there had been no time for healing. Ramón had spent every spare minute with Señorita Sandoval who quickly became Consuelo and they stayed on and on.

The hurt had run deep and at Christmas she had not come, making the excuse to her mother that her father was unwell and needed her, but in the long summer holiday after her last days at school she had returned to Venezuela.

She was just eighteen and very vulnerable, her childhood

admiration and awe with Ramón blossoming into a timid and frightening love that had grown over the year of their separation. She had almost wept aloud in anguish to find Doña Barbara firmly settled for one of her prolonged stays, Carmen and the beautiful Consuelo Sandoval with her. It did not need any imagination to realise that the twelve months had seen the relationship between Ramón and the beautiful Venezuelan girl grow.

Meriel had endured dinner in their company, painfully aware of her still too slender body at the side of the voluptuous Consuelo. The dusky pink dress that her father had bought her was daring for her, off the shoulder and tight at the bodice, but it had felt childish at the side of the gowns of her mother and their guests.

After dinner they had moved to the *sala*, their talk excluding her as it had always done, and she had escaped into the flower-scented air of the night, walking along the low veranda almost to the end, out of sight of them, wishing with all her heart that she had broken her promise and never returned.

She had not heard Ramón come out until his hand had touched her shoulder, making her start guiltily.

'You are nervous as a kitten,' he observed softly. 'You have a guilty secret?'

'N-no.' She turned her face but he turned it back towards him looking down at her in the moonlight.

'I am sorry that I did not meet you,' he offered. 'I was very busy.'

With Consuelo Sandoval, she thought miserably, but she managed a smile.

'It doesn't matter, I got here, as you see.'

He looked at her steadily and then took her hand, drawing it through his arm.

'Come and look at your foal. He is a baby no longer and also it is time that he had a name.'

'It's dark!' She had tried to withdraw her hand, frightened by her own heartbeats, but he merely tightened his grip.

'There is a moon like a lantern over the *llanos*,' he observed drily, 'and I know where he will be. Every night at this hour I give him a treat. He waits by the fence.' He withdrew his other hand from the pocket of his dinner-jacket, opening his palm and tossing up a few cubes of sugar. 'He will be there, greedy for his sweets and clear for us to see.'

It had been hard to enthuse over the horse, although he had enchanted her with his velvet nostrils and liquid dark eyes, and, his treat over, he had wandered away. But Ramón seemed content to linger, his foot on the bottom bar of the fence as they watched the horse retreat into the shadows.

'At Christmas you did not come,' he said quietly, his face strong and harsh in the moonlight as he gazed across the paddock.

'No.' She offered no excuse, knowing that her mother would have explained.

'I thought that perhaps you would not come again,' he observed in the same quiet voice.

'I promised you . . .' she began and he turned, his back to the fence, looking down at her, his features in the shadow, the moonlight full on her face.

'That is the only reason that you are here?'

'Yes.' She looked down, her lashes shadowy on her cheeks. 'No one would have missed me.'

'It is unusual to hear an unkind word on your lips,' he told her softly. 'Manuel would have missed you, he missed you at Christmas. Your mother too would have been unhappy.'

'I don't really think so,' she ventured, 'but I'm sorry about Manolito.'

'I too would have missed you.' He lifted his hand and raised her face, and although the moonlight made it difficult she could see the brilliant intensity of his eyes. She could find no words to say, her mouth suddenly dry, her skin hot.

He too said nothing more but his hand moved over her

face softly and slowly, tracing the contours, shaping her dark brows, cupping the pale bloom of her cheeks. She was spellbound, a tight pain flowering inside her as languor flooded her limbs, and when he drew her towards him she moved with soft acquiescence.

Still he said nothing, his hands smoothing her hair, exploring the shell of her ears, moving down her slender neck and across her bare shoulders, his eyes following the movements of his hands until she whispered with an unknown longing and his arms closed around her.

'A pale and beautiful rose, blooming in the moonlight.'

His voice was thick and deep and he moved until he leaned against the fence, drawing her tightly against him before taking her lips with a deep groan of need.

There was a searing, yearning response inside her and his arms tightened as he felt it, his lips urging hers to part and allow him to invade the sweet moisture of her mouth. When he lifted his head, her breath was a frantic sobbing in her throat and he trailed his lips over her shoulders and along the slender white column of her neck, closing her eyes with light kisses, his hands gentle and coaxing on her nape.

'You are afraid of me, Meriel?' he breathed huskily.

'No—no.' She gasped out the words, her head thrown back as his mouth caressed her skin.

'I am dangerous, though,' he warned her in a low voice, his breathing harsh. 'I look at you and there is a hunger in me like that of *el tigre* out across the moonlit plains.'

'I don't care!' She wound her arms around his neck and he buried his face in her hair.

'This is what you want?' he asked in a strained voice, every muscle taut like an animal ready to spring into life. 'This—and this?' His lips searched her jawline and moved relentlessly down to the shadowy hollow at the base of her throat.

'Yes! Oh, yes!' She was wildly happy even though she had lied, because she was afraid. She was afraid of the power of his body, the intensity of his kisses, the thick alien huskiness of his voice and the feeling that like *el tigre* he would devour her. But her trembling body clung to him and his kisses brought her to heated, singing life.

'You are a child, barely eighteen, and I am almost twenty-nine,' he warned, seemingly unable to stop his lips from kissing her, his hands from tracing the soft contours of her body.

'I'm not a child!' she cried, a new fear suddenly striking her. 'I know what I want!'

'Last year, you wanted a career, a hard-selling, fast-talking job in the world of the press,' he reminded her. 'This year you want me?' He drew back and looked into her eyes, seeing the tears shining on her lashes. She shook her head in an agony of frustration, trying to move close again, but he held her away, gazing at her in the moonlight with dark, glittering eyes.

'I've always wanted you,' she whispered brokenly, begging him to understand. 'Last year, I didn't know . . . I couldn't explain . . . But inside, I've always known that . . .'

'And so have I,' he breathed thickly. 'I have always known that one day you would be like a dangerous trap and that I would walk into it foolishly and willingly.'

He pulled her back to him, moulding her to the hard planes of his body, leaving her in no doubt of his desire, kissing her until she sobbed his name against his lips, their breath as one. Her body was shocked by the hard thrust of him against her but she couldn't move away, a new and terrifying delight surging through her at the power of him that she had never before even thought of, and he seemed to know her mind.

'You have never before been held like this,' he muttered thickly, his lips searching her face. 'You are shocked by my desire.' She wanted to deny it but in any case she could not because his mouth was hot on her bare shoulders, the dress moved aside as he caressed the silken rise of her breast with kisses that burned. 'I want you, Meriel,' he breathed against her skin. His lips were feverish against her neck, against her mouth as his hands shaped her body, trapping her against the frightening strength of his thighs. 'I have been hungry for a long, long time. A tantalising glimpse of you and then you are gone, and each time you return you are more beautiful.' He raised his head and looked down at her in the moonlight, his eyes roaming hotly over her shoulders, the frantic rise and fall of her breast now only partly concealed. 'So very beautiful,' he breathed huskily. 'So—perfect!'

His words thrilled her even more and she wound her arms tightly around his neck, her softness lying willingly and eagerly against him, her body inviting and freely offered, her fears stilled by the exciting power of the man who held her tightly.

'I don't want you to be hungry,' she sobbed against his lips. 'I want to belong to you—now. I've always belonged to you, Ramón!'

Her voice seemed to bring him out of the frenzy of passion that had him in its grip and he groaned aloud, putting her away from him and drawing harsh breath into his lungs as if gasping for life.

'Go back to the house, Meriel,' he said in a shaken voice, turning away and leaning against the fence, his arms along the top bar, his head dropping forward.

'Ramón!' She wanted to reach out and touch him but she dared not. She was afraid of so many things, of rejection, of scorn at her ready acceptance of his passion, but most of all, she was afraid of that passion that would sweep her under its waves like a small shell in an angry sea.

'Go back, Meriel,' he repeated tightly. 'Go to bed— please! I will see you tomorrow.'

She went back on trembling legs, half understanding his sudden withdrawal, half afraid to meet him the next day— as well she might have been.

Next morning she ate breakfast early and alone, still trembling and anxious, and her anxiety did not lessen at the sight of Ramón, dressed for riding as he strode into the breakfast-room.

'Ramón!' Consuelo appeared like a beautiful genie but Ramón hardly spared her a glance.

'I am taking Meriel riding,' he said in a taut voice. 'I need to talk to her in private. I will see you later, Conseulo.' He looked at Meriel with tight lips. 'Get dressed to ride,' he ordered. Whatever he had to say was not good, his looks made that very obvious.

They rode towards the river hut when they were still far off he reined in and caught her reins too.

'I absolve you of your promise,' he said quietly with a flat finality in his voice.

'I   I don't understand.' She looked at him with wide eyes and he met her gaze squarely.

'You do, Meriel, I forced a promise from you that you would return to Venezuela for good, you have returned. Now I give you back the promise. You are free.'

She stared at him with widening grey eyes, a chill racing over her skin as she said accusingly,

'You don't want me! Last night you said . . .!'

'Of course I want you!' he bit out impatiently. 'I would not be human if I did not, but it is an impossible situation, ridiculous and dangerous. In the first place, you are a child. In the second place, you are my stepsister.'

'I'm not a child!' she interrupted wildly. 'And I'm no relation to you, no more a relation than Señorita Sandoval!'

'You are a child!' he ground out harshly, adding in a taunting voice that had her face paling to a dead white, 'Consuelo is a woman and does not readily offer herself after a few kisses. I am as much a male animal as *el tigre* and part of the pleasure is in the hunting. You do not need to be hunted, you have been ready to fall into my arms and into my bed since you were little more than a child. You are still a child! What do you imagine would have been the result if I had accepted your ready offer last night? I will tell you. Soon, very soon I would have been bored out of my mind!'

She stared at him in a state of shock that held her fast to the spot. He had been cool, distant, uninterested, but never had he been cruel as he was now. His dark eyes narrowed at her deep stillness. He was waiting for some comment but she was unable to speak.

'You are English, Meriel,' he continued in a hard voice

when it became clear that she would not utter a word. 'You are English in your appearance, your habits and in your heart. Venezuela is not the place for you, it never has been. You will be better with your father in England, with your own kind.'

It hit her like the lash of a whip and she flinched with the cruel shock of it but she was accustomed to rejection, well used to being an outsider in this land and in the *hacienda*, and she never answered. She turned and rode quietly back to the *hacienda* and Ramón did not follow. During the day he left for the mines and she did not see him again.

CHAPTER FOUR

It was after midnight when the sound of Manuel's screams awoke Meriel. She had been in a very deep sleep and the screams that rang through the quiet of the house were violent and shocking, making her grab her robe hastily and race from her room.

Ramón, still dressed, was also on his way and they met in the doorway of Manuel's room as Meriel pushed open the door and ran white-faced into the darkness.

'For God's sake! Why isn't there a light on in here?' she demanded, feeling for the switch, her hand brushing Ramón's as he found it first.

'I would think—Carmen,' he muttered, blinking in the sudden light that flooded the room and turning worried eyes to the bed where Manuel knelt against the pillows, awake now and sobbing wildly.

'Shh! It was only a dream.' Meriel knelt beside him and pulled him into her arms, rocking him against her, his face at her breast. 'You're awake now and I am here, so is Ramón. It was only a dream.'

For a while he sobbed loudly and unrestrainedly and she let him, rocking back and forth with him in a soothing rhythm, her arms tightly around the shaking body as Ramón looked on helplessly.

'I miss them, Merry,' Manuel whispered against her as the violent weeping at last eased. 'I will always be lonely.'

'No.' She raised his face and wiped his tears away, looking into his eyes. 'Once I thought that too, when I was much older than you, but it was not true. Life is very exciting and there are many people who will love you and care for you for ever.'

'Is that what happened to you, Merry?' he sniffed,

looking up at her with dark unhappy eyes.

'Of course, Manolito.' She smiled down at him and hugged him close. 'Nothing is for ever no matter how much it hurts at the time. I thought that when I was very young but I was wrong. There was someone to love me and now I'm very happy and I have you too.'

'You'll not go, Merry.'

'No. I'll be here until you don't need me any more.'

'Good.' He settled down into bed again. 'That means for ever so I can go to sleep, now that you have promised.'

It sounded like Ramón and for a wild moment she felt her heart turn uneasily as she raised her eyes, almost as if commanded to meet the dark gaze of her stepbrother.

'What do you expect?' he asked with a shrug. 'He is an Ortiga. Do not worry, when he is restored to normality he will no doubt absolve you from your promise and allow you to return to your—happiness.'

She stared at him with angry eyes, fighting the rush of pain, and he turned to the door, motioning her before him, leaving the light and closing Manuel, now asleep, into the quiet of his room.

'That was bad,' he said in a worried voice. 'I had thought that perhaps the worst had passed.'

'Have you seen him every time he's had one of these nightmares?'

He nodded grimly and she felt a burst of anger. So much for Carmen who even now had made no appearance.

'I'm getting a hot drink. Do you want one?' she asked abruptly, and he smiled tiredly, turning with her as she walked towards the kitchen.

'That would be nice, I think.' He glanced at his watch. 'I had forgotten the hour. We will perhaps not leave so early in the morning. We will stay overnight in Caracas instead.'

'Thank you for consulting me,' she murmured sarcastically, flicking on the light in the gleaming modern kitchen. 'That means that I'll have to pack a bag for Manolito and myself. Still, it means more shopping time.'

She busied herself with heating milk and getting cups from the high cupboards as Ramón perched on the edge of the table, watching and saying nothing.

'You realise,' she said at last into the tightening silence, 'that the probable reason for the renewed nightmares is the idea of flying tomorrow!'

'I know it,' he said quietly. 'It is, however, necessary.'

'It could have waited, I think,' she suggested tartly, her eyes flashing to his. 'A few more weeks would have made all the difference to him.'

'When you were learning to ride and fell with frustrating frequency from your mount,' he reminded her, 'I put you back at once into the saddle. Do you not remember why?'

'Yes,' she sighed, giving him best as usual.

'A fear can only grow,' he stated, 'and it is worse to imagine than to face. Manuel must fly otherwise he is here like a person marooned in a sea of tall grass. The journeys are too long without a plane and one day he will run the *hacienda* and all the business of the Ortigas. He will run it alone if I do not marry. There is not the time for long and tiresome journeys by road.'

She nodded. She didn't want to think about the time when Ramón would marry. For almost seven years she had pushed him out of her mind, but within one day the old magic, the old yearning had started to eat into her again and she was trapped securely. She could not leave Manolito, and to stay would only weaken her resolve to treat Ramón as a cold, uncaring stranger.

The flight to Caracas the following day was after all uneventful. Ramón flew the plane himself and Meriel sat in the back with Manuel, his fingers tightly grasping hers, leaving Carmen to sit beside Ramón. Gradually, the tight grip had slackened and she saw her brother looking more and more out of the window, his interest growing as his fear lessened, and once again, she bowed to Ramón's superior knowledge and common sense.

Today, she was the one who felt marooned, trapped by Manuel's need and the promise she had made. It was odd that from being so locked out and forlorn, the demands on her were now demands of love. There was Manolito who wished her to stay here for ever, there was her father who had not remarried although he was only in his late forties and who cherished every moment with her, and then there was Stewart Mackensie who wanted to marry her.

Her eyes ran over Ramón who sat in front of her, flying the light plane with the competence he showed in everything, and she realised with a sinking, sickening feeling that she was secretly feasting her eyes on him, as drawn to him now as she had ever been, her yearning more painful now that it was the desire of a grown woman.

She forced her eyes away and looked across the *llanos*. What was Doña Barbara like now—almost seven years later? She had always been uncompromisingly straight and stiff, sternly unbending in her superior glances. Had she softened? Meriel doubted it, Carmen had grown more unspeakable with the passing of the years.

And what had become of Consuelo Sandoval? She had been in no doubt when Ramón had rejected her that he had intended to marry the Venezuelan girl, that his desire for her had been only a moment of moonlit madness. Still, he had said that there had been plenty of women in his life while she had been away. Her hands clenched and she dragged her thoughts free of him, realising only too well that she didn't want to imagine other women in his arms, welcoming his kisses.

She was afraid, as fearful as she had ever been in this land. She needed to draw on her years in England and her independence to strengthen her resolve to dislike Ramón and somehow take Manolito away from here. The time could not come soon enough.

As they drove along the Avenida Libertador towards the Caracas Hilton, Meriel found that in spite of her many worries and growing misery a sort of bubbling excitement was growing inside her. For the rest of the day and for much of the next day she would be here in Caracas, in the thriving dynamic city that lifted the spirits, its streets wide and splendid, filled with irrepressible Venezuelans and tourists from all over the world. Carmen had gone, reluctantly and with many uneasy backward glances, but nevertheless she had gone, and as they sat in the car that Ramón had hired, Meriel saw Manolito's spirits rising to meet the occasion, his eyes like saucers as he twisted his head from side to side, trying to see everything at once, questions and comments pouring from him in never-ending streams.

Ramón too was all Venezualen today, his expression amused as he listened to Manuel, his eyes softly mocking when they fell on Meriel, and once more she found herself going under in the tide of feeling that swept over her whenever she was close to her stepbrother.

'How soon can we shop?' she asked as breathlessly as Manuel, both anxious to know and anxious too to have the dark eyes a little more cool. She needed all the help she could get.

'When we are settled if you feel up to it,' he said easily. 'This afternoon I have an appointment that cannot be put off as it is the reason for this visit, but later, or tomorrow, I can take you wherever you wish to go.'

'No!' She felt a hot burst of colour when his eyes momentarily left the busy highway and glanced in astonishment at her sharp refusal. 'I—I mean you don't have to bother. Leave Manolito to me and then you'll be free to get on without too much strain.'

'How very kind,' he said softly. 'I have arranged to meet my visitor in the suite that we have booked at the hotel. You are suggesting then that afterwards I lie back on the settee and put my feet up while you brave the traffic of this teeming metropolis?'

'Why not? I'm sure you work too hard. You—you could

perhaps get a little sleep in. You looked really tired last night.'

'I do not know whether to be touched by your kindness to me or deeply suspicious,' he said, bursting into quiet laughter. 'I cannot think offhand what mischief you could be planning. I think I have covered all exigencies in that direction, having seen the sort of wilful person you have become, but even so, you do not know Caracas and I would hate to lose you both.'

'I live in one of the biggest and busiest cities in the world!' Meriel retorted. 'In any case, I can take a taxi wherever I want to go and I assume that the taxi drivers know Caracas.'

He nodded, still amused and thoughtful. 'Very well, I will take your advice. After my meeting I will rest. I only hope that you will not be falling asleep in my arms tonight when we dine. The dancing here is good,' he added as he pulled into the hotel car park. 'We will make the most of it while we are here.'

'Oh, I don't think ...' Meriel began anxiously, the thought of being in Ramón's arms for any reason at all, not to her liking.

'Thinking will not be necessary,' he assured her firmly. 'I have already done the thinking. I have agreed to your suggestion, I hope that you will also agree to my plans.'

'Will I be allowed to watch television in my room as usual, Ramón?' Manuel put in excitedly. 'I normally do when you come here and go downstairs to dinner and to dance.'

'Naturally, everyone to his own pleasure,' Ramón assured him reasonably. 'You think that you are up to it? You seem to be earmarked for an afternoon's shopping.'

'I'll be fine! I'll not be tired. You promised, Ramón!'

'I did, and promises must be kept,' Ramón answered, his eyes darting a glance of pure mischief at Meriel.

She was still worriedly mulling that over in her mind when later she pushed her way through the crowds with

Manuel's hand firmly in her own, her bag seemingly full of money that Ramón had quietly but insistently pressed on her. She too had made a promise to Manolito and she was as incapable of breaking her promises as was Ramón, he had trained her too well for that. Also she had been quietly but startlingly shocked to find that Ramón and Manuel had a life together that she knew nothing of. They came to Caracas together, it seemed. She had never thought of that, had never thought that they would have any common ground, that Ramón would have either the time or the inclination to drag a boy with him to the city. He had protected her because she was an outsider and lonely but it seemed that after all, in spite of her thoughts to the contrary, Ramón treated Manuel as his brother and cared about him, was lenient with him.

The thoughts were pushed to the back of her mind as she took Manuel from shop to shop, modernising his wardrobe and gleefully smartening him in a way that would be anathema to Doña Barbara and Carmen. A young man of the world.

She said this to him when they had at last finished and Manuel grinned widely, pleased with the purchases and still filled with energy. On the way too, she had bought herself a gown for the evening. Her clothes were not suitable for any dinner and dance at this de-luxe hotel where world-famous artistes entertained guests in the rooftop supper club, and Ramón had made no mention of their hotel when they had left the *hacienda*. Spending some of his money didn't trouble her at all, curiously enough; she would have been more troubled if she had been forced to appear beside him looking shabby.

It was getting late and she glanced at her watch.

'Just time for one more thing before we meet Ramón for tea,' she said, briskly darting into a shop beside them and pointing out to Manuel the coloured jeans and T-shirts on display. 'One more for the road?'

'*Sí*, if it pleases you, Merry.' Manuel took off his tie and prepared once again to try on clothes, his eyes amused when he looked at her.

'Yes—well.' She didn't like the way her heart leapt when she saw the likeness between Manuel and Ramón.

When they returned to the hotel in a taxi, their purchases stacked on the seat beside the driver, they had a minute to observe each other's apparel. They had kept on the latest garments, Manuel at last calling a halt to endless dressing and undressing and Meriel because she felt in some queer way defiant, a perverse desire to shock Ramón surging through her.

Manuel was all modern youth, tight blue jeans and a bright yellow T-shirt that contrasted splendidly with his black hair, new sneakers on his feet, but it was the T-shirt that was designed for shock. 'Hot shot.' The words were emblazoned across his chest and Meriel dissolved into laugher when she thought of the expression on Carmen's face if she should ever see him like this. Manuel too was openly laughing as he gazed at her. In red jeans, equally tight, her feet in red and white trainers, she looked for the first time in her life impish and just slightly outrageous, the four-inch word across the front of her T-shirt holding the eye and drawing attention to her round, high breasts. 'Help!' It stood out in stark black against the white and there was no ignoring it.

'I think that help is what we shall both need when Ramón sees these things,' Manuel warned, but she was not to be intimidated right now.

'Nonsense!' We'll meet him for tea as arranged. We'll only be a couple of minutes late.'

'I think that perhaps you are making a mistake, Meriel,' Manuel said, growing a little anxious, but she grinned at him widely, his greatly loved sister, and he smiled the slow smile that Ramón could tear at her heart with and said nothing more.

She did wonder whether or not she should have taken his advice, though, when they presented themselves at the door of the rather splendid tea-room in the hotel and were stopped by as very firm but very polite waiter.

'I regret, *señorita*, that it is necessary for the young man to be in a little more formal dress to take tea here and also, regrettably, ladies are expected to wear a skirt or dress, or some such thing.'

'But we're staying here!'

'Ah! Very good! Then I will see that your order is prepared while you change for tea.' The smile was genuine, but firm.

'I'll do no such thing!' Her newer dynamic personality surfaced and Meriel dug in. 'We are taking tea with someone and we are already five minutes late!'

'*Señorita*, I regret but . . .'

'They are with me, Marcelo, in spite of their odd appearance.' Ramón, elegant in grey slacks and grey silk shirt, his cream silk tie a perfection of its own, walked easily towards them and took Meriel's arm. 'My brother you surely remember and as to my wife, I am afraid that she is English. The English love to play pranks and I fear that this one is directed at me. There are few guests in the tea-room at this hour. Forgive their unruly appearance on this occasion.'

'Señor Ortiga, I understand, I did not know that you . . . it will be quite all right, Señora Ortiga, my apologies.'

Meriel was hustled away with ease in a charming way that looked as if she was being escorted to her table like a queen, but the iron grip on her arm told her that Ramón was not particularly amused. Scenes were not in his line. They were not in her line either and she wondered what had come over her.

'The English also have an overrated opinion of themselves,' Ramón added darkly as the waiter departed. 'They ignore the customs of others and delight in drawing attention to themselves, which is not a very pleasant way of conducting one's affairs.'

His eyes fell on her T-shirt, lingering on the quickening

rise and fall of her breasts and the word emblazoned across the front. 'I am greatly surprised that you did not also buy a nice hat with "Kiss me quick" written across the front of it. You are surely in an outfit that slightly lacks something.'

Manuel smothered a burst of laughter and drank his tea with a solemn dignity that Meriel wished she could copy. She was as shy and red-faced now as she had ever been when Ramón called her to order.

'Why—why did you tell that man that I was your wife?' she demanded in a low voice, Manuel trying very hard to look as if he was totally deaf.

'How else do you imagine I was going to get you in here and rescue both you and the waiter from the embarrassing situation that you had created?' he asked coolly.

'There was no need for him to refuse us entry!' she began hotly but he silenced her with cold eyes and a sharp reprimand.

'The rules are not his. He is merely the waiter. The rules are for the comfort and peace of mind of the other guests. I would very much doubt if anyone would think to appear in the public rooms in a bikini but perhaps there are others about with little discrimination. The rules are to keep them on the right tracks. It is very bad form to embarrass a person who is merely doing his job but perhaps you do not know that.'

She was trembling now with nerves and her bag fell to the floor, spilling the contents close to the table, and she bent quickly to retrieve it, fumbling in her anxiety. Ramón too bent quickly, his strong capable hands rapidly replacing the make-up, money and sun-glasses that had spread themselves across the floor.

'If you tell me what kind of help you need I will try to oblige,' he said quietly, below the hearing of Manuel. 'The message is for me, is it not?'

She shot up very rapidly indeed and when next she risked a glance at him he was calmly drinking tea, no expression on his face but deep in his eyes a thoughtful speculation.

'Did you buy anything for yourself?' he asked pleasantly when they were at last back in the luxury of the apartment that he had rented and Manuel had disappeared to his own room to begin the job of unpacking his new clothes.

'Yes, I bought a dress for this evening. As you didn't see fit to point out to me that we would be dining in a splendid place, I brought nothing suitable with me.'

'Very good.' He leaned against her bedroom door as she strode away from him. 'That was very wise thinking. I hope however that the dress is not embroidered with anxious words.'

She did not answer and he strolled uninvited into the room as she turned angrily to request that he leave.

'The little scene down there was for my benefit, was it not, Meriel?' he asked quietly, standing near to her. 'I was to be put in my place in a defiant and childish manner?'

'No.' She looked down her lashes covering her flushed cheeks. 'I just didn't think. It was stupid really but when the waiter said we couldn't come in I . . .'

'You felt once again in your life—excluded—but this time your new-found security and hard-headed salesperson attitude surfaced automatically!'

She stared at him, almost frightened by his astute recognition of her mood when she had confronted the waiter, and he smiled softly.

'You see? I know you. I know you better than anyone in the world knows you.' He lifted his hand and began to trace the words across her breasts with one tantalising finger. 'An intriguing message. What deep and hidden instinct made you choose this particular word, I wonder?'

Almost unable to breathe as his finger reached the rise of her breast and moved across the swollen mound to the hard tightening centre, she drew back with a gasp of alarm and he smiled slowly, his eyes widening into intent consideration.

'Is there another message on the back?' he enquired softly. 'I confess that I have neglected to look, as the front is so absorbing.' He reached for her shoulders and turned her easily because she had no resistance in her body and he knew it. 'I'm disappointed,' he breathed softly, pulling her against him, his breath warm on her face as he bent to whisper to her. 'I had hoped that there was another message for me. "I want you, Ramón", because you do, don't you, Meriel?'

'No!' Stung into life, she pulled free, but she could not face him and she heard his soft laughter as he walked out of the room.

'You have never been able either to lie or conceal your feelings,' he said with amusement. 'You will tell me the words without the aid of a written message before you leave my country.'

He closed the door quietly and she pulled off the T-shirt and threw it to the ground. She had been called to order and punished in the most cruel way that he could find, and her fear grew as she realised again that he could almost read her soul.

She dressed for dinner later in a thoughtful mood, trying to be as she had become and not as she had always been in this land. It was no use ducking the issue, hiding from the truth: she was still in love with Ramón, more in love with him than she had been at eighteen. All that six years had done was to heighten her senses, her awareness of him, and she could tell herself any stories she liked, embroider any incident of coldness and cruelty, it made little difference.

Fighting him was so clearly a waste of time. He would always win, and her new-found confidence ebbed away every time he looked at her. There was only one way to defeat him—to be his stepsister, to rely on his not forgotten protection and his lingering desire to help her.

She knew him as well as he knew her. He would call her to order, scorn her, hurt her, but if anyone else attempted the same treatment he would spring forward to her defence like the jaguar of the plains. He had protected her from the accident, dismissed Carmen at her request, bowed to her demands to refurbish Manuel's wardrobe. He was her stepbrother still and committed to his duties so that she would always be under his protection because she was a small satellite on the very edge of the mighty orbit of the Ortigas. She might be unwanted, excluded, but she was real and not to be insulted, hurt or ignored by anyone who did not remotely touch their lives; only they had the right to exclude her and her position was a determined factor.

She gave a final flick to her hair, smooth and silky, deep gold in the lamplight, her heavy fringe swept to one side. The dress she had bought was not quite glamorous but it suited her, made her feel good, the white organza floating over a pale green satin skirt, the bodice tight and low, a fairytale froth of white. She smoothed on a pale lipstick, hopeful that the dress would help her to play the game she had planned, a game to keep Ramón at arm's length until she could defeat him and finally get away to London and her settled life.

'You look lovely, Merry!' Manuel was all admiration when she went to say goodnight and found him perched in bed reading, the television control at the ready in his hand.

'Beautiful!' Ramón's voice echoed the praise and she turned to find him standing in the doorway watching her.

'Well, thank you!' She smiled brilliantly at them both. 'It's nice to have such an appreciative family.'

'You look very much like a bride,' Ramón murmured as they went to the lift and she forced an impish smile to her shaking lips.

'Let's hope that the waiter from the tea-room is on duty upstairs tonight then. He'll believe your story more readily if he sees the bridal gown.'

He said nothing and she hoped that she had not overplayed her hand. Her heart sank as fast as the lift when she realised that they were going down and not up, but Ramón hushed her queries.

'One moment only. Wait for me here.'

He strode into the foyer and out of sight, leaving her by the lift as he went towards the expensive arcade of shops that catered for the wealthy guests at the hotel, but it was only when they were again in the lift, this time ascending, that he produced the small Cartier box and withdrew a thin golden chain with an exquisite opal hanging like a raindrop arrested in time from its centre.

'Some say that opals are unlucky,' he remarked softly, 'but against your skin it is a small drop of moonlight.'

He fastened it around her neck, letting the opal fall into the shadows between her breasts.

'It—it's beautiful. It must have cost a fortune! Ramón—why did you . . .?'

'You are tastefully dressed. I am enhancing the taste,' he said mockingly, adding in a quiet voice, 'though if you were suddenly to don a hat with "Kiss me quick" written across it, I would be happy to oblige.'

He stood over her, his hands on both sides of her, resting against the panelling of the lift, trapping her securely.

'I'm glad to see that you're in a good mood,' she managed to smile, frantically trying to keep up her sisterly act. 'I always know that you're in a good mood when you're teasing me.'

'Is that what I'm doing?' he asked, looking down at her wryly.

Their table was near the dance-floor but in an intimate corner and she was really grateful. She wanted no interested onlookers to see her playing the little sister. And play it she did until she was exhausted. As one course followed another and as they watched the floor-show she chattered away happily about anything that came into her head, her eyes over-bright, her lips constantly smiling until the effect threatened to bring about her complete physical collapse.

And Ramón played along with her, sliding into the role he had played for years but this time with no frowns, only charm and wit. She was thankful for the brief respite when later he stood and invited her to dance, at least she could keep quiet out there and catch her breath, think up some new topic of conversation. Her skin was flushed with her efforts, her facial muscles stretched tight with the need to keep on smiling, and out on the dimness of the dance-floor he took her into his arms, moving to the slow rhythm of the dance.

'Peace at last!' he murmured, laughter in his voice. 'Now I can rest from the utter exhaustion that playing your game has brought me.'

'I'm not playing any game!' She looked up, forcing her tired mouth to smile again, but he shook his head despairingly and pulled her shining head to his shoulder, locking her against him.

'Please, Meriel!' he murmured in amusement. 'You have tired me out. I cannot keep pace with your acting ability. I cannot match your lines as you frantically play the part of my small defenceless sister.'

'I am your sister!' she muttered. 'Well, your stepsister.'

He tilted her face and looked down at her with dark, unreadable eyes before pushing her head gently back to his shoulder.

'You are a slender, frightened, beautiful—idiot,' he averred softly. 'Rest, before you overdo it and shatter into a thousand glittering pieces. You are generating enough energy and brilliance to light up the whole of Caracas.'

What was the use? With a sigh she stayed where she was, feeling a sort of hopeless comfort when his hand began to massage to tight muscles of her neck.

'Silly child,' he commented softly. 'You have gained a few interesting curves, a little self-confidence but basically you are still the same—foolish.'

She was too tired to argue anyway. With Ramón it was possible to cram in a lot of living in one day. She had brought up a new idea and had it knocked down after he had allowed her to exhaust herself and behave like a halfwit. Right at this moment she had run completely out of ideas—maybe tomorrow ...

She yawned tiredly and found him grinning at her as she looked up.

'You had better go to bed, I think, like a good girl, like the sort of girl you are playing,' he observed, leading her off the floor. 'I will see you safely up and then come back to join the grown-up ladies.'

There had been plenty of them, watching him all evening, and he did exactly what he had said, he went back down, but she was too tired to care. She let her dress fall to the floor, wiped off her make-up and fell into bed.

CHAPTER FIVE

NEXT morning, Meriel awoke to the touch of a cool hand on her shoulder, irritation in her that she had been forced into wakefulness when she was still so tired. For a second she was disorientated, back in her London flat, certain that her alarm had not rung and that therefore this was a great liberty that someone was taking to bring her out of her pleasantly dreamy world.

Realisation of her surroundings came with an embarrassing rush however when she opened her eyes and turning her face sideways, found herself looking into the amused, dark eyes of her stepbrother.

'Oh!' She spun round on to her back and struggled up, sinking back under the sheets with equal speed when she realised that her only covering seemed to be the glowing opal pendant that still hung warm and beautiful between her breasts.

'Ay ay ay!' he said softly, his smile growing. 'Now I know how the opal should be worn.' He reached across and lifted the precious stone, his fingers brushing her flesh as she lay with the sheets tightly around her, only her bare shoulders a focus for his laughing eyes. 'It is still warm,' he murmured, watching her flushed and anxious face. 'I really believe that it has picked up an extra glow from you.' He dangled it on the chain, away from her neck and then lowered it slowly back into place, watching it slide across her heated skin and resume its place in the deep secret hollow.

'We leave very soon,' he said with suddenly tight and unsmiling face. 'I have still many things to do. You told me to leave Manuel to you and I am holding you to that. Get up and resume your duties.'

'All right, I'll be up the moment you go. Thank you for

waking me.' She wasn't quite sure what had wiped the smile from his eyes but there was no doubt that the teasing mood had gone as if it had never been there at all.

'It took very little effort,' he said stiffly. 'I have wakened you before in your life, usually to invite you to ride across the *llanos* before my day became too busy. Today I am inviting you to take up your share of the responsibility of your brother.'

He stood up and lifted the lovely dress from the floor where she had left it the night before. For a second he looked at it, his mind clearly far away, and then he turned brilliantly intent eyes on her before tossing the dress on to the bed and walking to the door.

'Breakfast in ten minutes,' he warned, 'no lingering!'

She got up at once as the door closed, still flushed and confused by the lingering touch of his hand on her skin, still filled with the anxiety that he had always been able to bring to her mind when he moved from what seemed to be one personality to another. She knew with a sinking heart that she was as defenceless against him as she had ever been and she was in no doubt why. He had always meant too much to her. Even as a child she had anxiously watched for Ramón's reactions to things, and now she loved him with a painful, pointless longing that would have to be fought.

'I thought that we'd be staying all day.' Meriel remarked as she sat down to a breakfast that had been served in their suite. Their table was on the veranda and she could look out across the city towards the hazy blue mountains. She became aware that Ramón had not answered, and Manuel hastily intervened as she glanced across at Ramón and saw that he was intent on the papers in his hand and was paying no attention whatever to either of them.

'We have trouble at one of the mines,' he said seriously. 'Ramón is taking us back and then going out there to sort it out.'

Somehow, his wording hit her hard. 'We have trouble at one of the mines.' The Ortiga mines. Manuel was already well on the way to being the Ortiga heir and absorbing the Ortiga attitude.

'You were very late up, Meriel,' he explained carefully as she stayed in gloomy silence. 'We waited breakfast for you and now it is very close to our time to leave.'

'I'm sorry,' she murmured absently. Meriel, not Merry as she had always been. Who needed her here anyway? For a long time her meetings with Manolito had been in England, not in his home background, and now she had discovered that not only did he get on well with Ramón, but that also he was the official spokesperson when Ramón didn't bother to answer.

'You must be disappointed, I know, Meriel, but I'm sure that you will be able to come another day.'

It was altogether too much and she shot him a horrified glance only to find to her relief that it was the anxious eyes of her dear Manolito looking at her and not the imperious Ortiga eyes she had dreaded for years.

'Watch it!' She narrowed her eyes and pointed a cautionary finger. 'You're beginning to sound like a very lordly person.'

'I try to copy Ramón,' he confessed, his face wreathed in smiles.

'A very dubious goal,' Ramón remarked quietly. He did not look up but he was clearly aware of what was going on around him and had simply not bothered to answer when she had spoken.

He spoke only briefly too on the flight back and in the car that Luis Silva had brought to meet them, and Meriel sat in the back with Manolito, fighting her own particular demons of the past and keeping her eyes firmly on either Manolito or the wide stretches of the plains.

'There is a call for you, Señorita Meriel, this very instant,' Rosita beamed as they entered the cool *hacienda*. 'It is a Señor Mackensie from England and he will call straight back because I was able to tell him that I could see the car approaching.' She was delighted with her ability to conduct a conversation in English and took all the shopping away with a very satisfied smile, Manuel excitedly talking to her and keeping pace with her quick little steps.

'Mackensie knows the telephone number here?' Ramón asked sharply as they left.

'Yes, he's my boss after all.'

'You are on leave! What reason does he have to interrupt your leave by telephoning?' He stood towering over her as if she were part of some conspiracy and there was no softness in him.

'I don't imagine that the Mackensie Press is about to go into liquidation just because I'm not there!' she answered in growing annoyance, stung by his demanding tone. 'I imagine that it's merely a private call, he's a friend too, you know. We're often together.'

The shrill ringing of the phone saved her from further argument and she dived to answer it.

'Meriel? You got back then!' It was so good to hear his easy, warm voice.

'Yes, we just got in.' Out of the corner of her eye she could see Ramón, still unmoving and openly listening, thinking no doubt that Stewart was about to cancel her leave.

'You sound edgy. Is everything all right?'

'Yes, darling. I'm perfectly fine.' She noticed Ramón stiffen with annoyance and knew that for once in her life she had struck gold. Let him worry about how long she was going to be here. Let him worry about her relationship with Stewart that might take her back at any time.

'Aha! You have an audience!' Stewart remarked astutely. 'I don't normally get that kind of encouragement. I'll overlook it this time, but don't push your luck or I'll be out there with a ring.'

'You know, you're really a wonderful man,' she said softly. 'You know what I want without having to be told. I'm not ready for a ring yet thought.'

She was wondering how her end of the conversation would sound to Ramón and evidently it sounded not to his liking because he strode along to his room and closed the door firmly.

'All clear,' she said with relief. 'What's up?'

'Nothing, my dear girl.' Stewart laughed. 'I just wondered if I could help.'

'You just did!' Meriel said wholeheartedly.

They talked for a while and then she went to her room, the small uplift that Stewart's call had given her draining away even before she reached her own door. Better to have Ramón's frowns than his newly acquired flirtatious behaviour, his amused assault on her peace of mind and new-found independence. She was in no doubt what he was doing. He was reducing her to the state she had been in when she had lived here in Venezuela so long ago, moulding her into a wary and weak personality that would acknowledge the Ortiga domination more readily. It hurt and it frightened her because she could not play games with Ramón.

He walked in almost behind her, briefcase in hand and a ferocious scowl on his face.

'I didn't hear you knock!' she said stiffly, turning on him at once.

'As I did not, it is not surprising!' he rasped. 'I wished to tell you that I am leaving and you are therefore in a position of some responsibility. I may be away a couple of days or I may be able to solve the problem at once—I do not know. Should I be delayed, I expect to find you here when I return. There may be the odd decision to make, however trivial, and Manuel is in your safe keeping. Do not desert him!'

'You know perfectly well that I won't!' she snapped angrily.

'Perhaps not,' he agreed, 'but I know that when England calls you are incapable of ignoring it. I knew that when you were a child. You have not changed very much.'

'I will not leave Manolito and, if you recall, I came immediately that you called me here!' she said hotly, anger boiling inside at his comments. She would have stayed for the rest of her life if he had asked her to. He had told her to go to her own kind and now with his usual ability to see only his own side of things he was accusing her of an obsessive attachment to England to the detriment of Manuel.

'Yes, you came,' he agreed quietly, 'but with obvious reluctance. I now understand why you were so reluctant. Inez, too, was greatly taken with Señor Mackensie. As she was rarely taken with anything at all, even her own children, he must have a great deal going for him. Remember, therefore, your duty here!'

He strode out, leaving her angry and miserable. His farewell words had been to remind her as usual of duty and also, it seemed, some veiled, unspoken threat.

It was easier to cope and be herself when he was gone and not likely suddenly to pop up wherever she happened to be. She enjoyed her day with Manuel as she had enjoyed her shopping with him the day before. There was no mistaking his attachment to her and they were very easy in each other's company, bedtime coming with regrettable swiftness as the deep blue night of the *llanos* drew around the *hacienda*. It was always odd to sleep here when Ramón was away and she realised as she tossed restlessly that she still felt like that. She remembered that as a child she had felt very vulnerable and alone when Ramón was not in the house or within call, and when he had been away on business she had waited heart in her mouth for his return, only to have her childish overtures of welcome met with an aloof nod most of the time. Not all the time, her honesty added. There had been times when she had been swept up into the air, her delighted eyes looking down into the warm darkness of his, and those days she had clung to like a brilliant chain of gold.

During her early days in England when she had finally left Venezuela she had puzzled over his unexpected and ardent lovemaking on that moonlit night, turning every action, every phrase over in her mind to find some explanation, but there had been none other than the one he had put forward himself. He had suddenly wanted her and had later come coldly and determinedly to his senses. If she were to think clearly about things, her life now and her treatment here were exactly what they would have been had she simply stayed to grow up in the *hacienda*. She would have been expected to be calm and businesslike, aware of duty and able to accept cool behaviour as part of her everyday life. Except for this tendency to get under her skin in the most masculine of ways, nothing had changed and there had to be some explanation for his sexual sniping. Ramón rarely did things with no end in view.

She was up early next morning feeling curiously rested and content, but her ease of mind suffered a severe blow when she walked into the breakfast room to find Ramón already there, looking as if he had never left the *rancho*.

'When did you get in?' She sat down and nodded pleasantly at the maid who brought her coffee, turning her startled gaze then upon Ramón.

'Last night,' he said quietly, 'or rather, early this morning.'

'I certainly never heard you!'

'That sounds rather like an accusation, although I am unsure what I am being accused of,' he said with raised brows. 'You were all asleep. I looked in on both you and Manuel.'

'I don't need to be checked off on your list like a prisoner!' she snapped, uneasy to think that she had lain asleep as Ramón looked at her.

'I wondered if all was well, that is all. I normally check my treasures when I have been away. I used to check your safety when you were a child, every night,' he added with emphasis. 'You did not know that, did you?'

'I'm not a child now!' she stated flatly, letting her temper rise to cover the fact that her cheeks were slowly reddening.

'True,' he agreed, watching her with intent narrowed eyes, 'but you are more elusive and need a careful eye on you even now.'

She couldn't think of anything to say but the day had not begun in a way that promised to be a joy. Her feeling of contentment had now gone completely and she waved away her breakfast, suddenly not hungry any more, as he continued to watch her silently for a few more seconds, his eyes on her lowered lashes and flushed cheeks.

'I have been giving a great deal of thought to the situation that we are in,' he said at last in the deepening silence. 'The obvious conclusion is that you remain here where Manuel can be with you constantly. It would be best if you resigned your position in England and simply stayed here at home.'

'I must be having hearing problems,' she said slowly, a numb cold beginning to seep into her body. 'I really don't think that I understood that any too well.'

'I imagine that you did,' he stated coolly, 'but I will repeat it. As we both know, Manuel needs you. Therefore it is a simple matter. Be here—permanently. There is absolutely no need for you to work. You have thrown my wealth in my face many times, why not make use of it? Anything you want can be yours. Manuel will be happy and things will settle down into normality.'

'I seem to have two choices here,' Meriel said carefully. 'I can begin to laugh hysterically or I can fly into a temper. For now, I'll try to keep calm and behave in the reasonable manner of the Ortigas—coldly and logically—you know the form,' she finished sarcastically. Her grip on her temper was very slight but she would not let him see how his off-hand suggestion had both hurt and frightened her. 'In the first place, there is Manuel. He is not as devastated as you led me to believe. I'm quite sure that you can cope with him without any help from me, although I'll stay as long as I can. In the second place, I do not work merely for money, which means less to me than you could possibly imagine. I work because I want to. I have a career, a way of life and it does not include this house, this country, or you!'

'Your place is here!' Anger flared across his face and he stood up to tower over her. 'Manuel needs you and you will remain!'

'He doesn't need me! He's perfectly normal! Grief passes

and provided you keep your abominable relatives away from him he will be back to being himself within a few days. The hurt will die slowly but it will die.'

'Is that what you found, Meriel?' he asked with angry quiet. 'Your grief died? You haven't in all the years of your absence yearned for the *llanos,* for the house where you lived, or for me?'

'No! I grew up with a loud bang! Staying here is not living, not for me!'

'And you do not care about Manuel?'

'You know damned well that I care about him, but you— Ramón—I hate you!' She was shouting now, hurt at his words and thoughts flooding her with pain, and she too stood to face him. 'I hate this place, this country, the very air that I'm forced to breathe here! There's no way that I'll even consider staying in Venezuela. The idea is the nearest thing to a nightmare that I can think of.'

'I intend that you shall stay!' he bit out harshly. 'If you do not agree to be reasonable, then I will personally telephone England and deal with your resignation!'

'Oh, no!' Meriel stopped shouting, a triumph coming into her face. 'There are some things, some people who are far beyond your reach in spite of the Ortiga power and wealth, and I am one of them. Stewart Mackensie will take my resignation from me and from no one else. You can telephone England right now and the first thing that he'll do is to phone right back to me. He's not just my boss, Ramón, he loves me and one day, I'm going to marry him!'

'I think not!' he said with soft menace, reaching forward and grasping her wrist tightly. 'You belong here and here is where you will stay!'

'I will stay for the rest of the week and then I leave,' she said coldly. 'I was prepared to stay as long as Manuel needed me, but now the situation is different. I've been a prisoner once in this house but I'll not creep back gently into that situation again. You may control the Ortiga wealth, the family, and temporarily, Manolito, but you do not control me! I was a fool to come back but I'll not make the same mistake ever again.'

A faint noise in the doorway caught their attention and they both turned united in a gasp of regret to see Manuel, his face white and strained as he looked at them with pain deep in his eyes. He had heard everything, or at least, he had heard enough to be quite clear in his mind that Meriel would leave and that there was enmity between the two people he loved most in the word.

'Manolito!' Meriel's unhappy cry halted him as he turned to leave and he stopped, slowly raising dark eyes to her face. 'Manolito, I'm sorry.' She walked across to him and knelt on the floor, looking up into his face. 'I didn't mean you to be hurt again, darling but I can't stay here now. You must release me from my promise, otherwise there'll be nothing but unhappiness.'

'I know.' He reached out and touched her hair, gently. 'I didn't mean to listen, Merry, but perhaps it's better. I know now. I didn't realise that . . .'

'Come with me, Manolito!' she said in an urgent voice. 'I'll take care of you and you like England. You can go to school there and be with other children instead of having a tutor. You'll not be lonely. We'll have fun. Come with me!'

He looked across at Ramón who had said not one word, had not cautioned or interrupted when Meriel had burst out with her sudden idea. For a second she watched as the two looked at each other and Ramón made no move to persuade the boy in any direction. She knew with certainty at that minute that if Manuel wished to go with her then Ramón would allow it and once again his attitude was a complete puzzle to her. She would have understood an outburst, had expected one. Instead, he was leaving the decision to a child.

'I cannot leave Venezuela and I cannot leave Ramón.' There was all the determination in Manuel's voice that she had heard all her life from the Ortigas. 'I am not lonely, Meriel, except that sometimes I am lonely for you. You are lonely here because you hate it but I love it most in the whole world. I have seen where you live and I understand.

Your promise is given back. I—I only wish that—that you did not also hate Ramón.'

He turned away and walked to his room and Meriel stayed where she was, still kneeling on the floor, her head bent in grief and defeat. He had always meant so very much to her, his love had been real when there had seemed to be no other happiness in her life. Memories of the delightful dark-eyed baby, the happy, cheerful toddler and the serious young brother who could suddenly burst into mischief filled her head and she knew that her anger and her outburst at Ramón had closed a chapter in her life very firmly and left her lonelier for it.

'What will you do now?' Ramón was beside her and to her surprise he was no longer angry. He lifted her to her feet and stood looking down at her with shuttered eyes.

'I'll go back to England.' She felt so weary that it seemed as if she had not slept at all. Defeat was the only feeling that she could recognise although there were others. Her hasty words were uppermost in her mind and she did not hate Ramón, she loved him and his indifference to that love left her cold and lost.

'You will go soon?' His determination to keep her seemed to have gone and she could understand that only too well. Now that Manolito knew her feelings he would not be likely to believe that she was staying willingly. It was all hopeless as it had always been hopeless.

'I may as well . . . perhaps tomorrow. Things will never be the same now.'

'It is you who have preached the sermon of healing,' he reminded her quietly. 'Do you then not believe in it after all? You think that there will be no healing between you and Manuel, between you and me?'

'Some things never heal,' she said quietly. 'I don't ever expect miracles.'

She walked away and he let her go, not attempting either to speak or follow as she made her way back to her room, beyond tears, numb with the latest misery. The guilt she felt was almost unbearable. It would have been better if she had never returned. Manuel would have recovered well enough because he loved Ramón and his home. Carmen too would eventually have been dispatched as Meriel knew deep down. Ramón's love for his brother would have permitted very little leeway as far as Carmen or anyone else was concerned and he ruled the family like some prince from the past, his wealth and authority keeping in check relatives who were more than twice his age. Her coming here had only brought heartache both to herself and to Manuel and the gulf between herself and Ramón was now wider and deeper than it had ever been.

For half an hour she paced her room trying to think of a way out of this mess but nothing came that was of any use. Only her early return to England would help in any way and she finally tidied her face and went to seek Manuel. He at any rate could not be left to suffer by himself.

There was no answer to her knock on his door and she imagined that he was by now somewhere with Ramón. To be sure however she carefully opened the door worried that he was weeping quietly and afraid that she should know. He was not there and her eyes skimmed the well known room with regret. She would never again sit here and talk to Manolito, never again come hurrying along at the excited call when he needed her.

He had been writing and she wandered over to the bed to look, a half-smile of sadness on her face as she recognised his rather childish handwriting and the large sheet of paper that was part of a lined block he had bought in Caracas. 'Dear Merry.' The sight of her own name startled her but as she read rapidly through it her face paled and she turned to the door in panic, one thought in her mind only, to find Ramón.

He was in his study, grim-faced and drawn-looking, but she could spare neither fear nor worry. All her fears were for Manuel.

'He's run away! Ramón! He's run away from the *hacienda*!'

She thrust the letter into his hand and turned to the door

but he was upon her before she had taken two steps.

'Wait!' His hand was uncompromising and secured her to his side as they read the letter together.

'I cannot bear to see you go and I do not want to hear you quarrel yet again with Ramón. I have decided to run away for a while until you are gone. When I grow up I will find you again and we will be happy.'

Ramón looked down into her white face for a second and then let her go.

'You will wait here,' he said firmly. 'I do not wish you to go roaming around the *llanos* searching for one small boy. I know him and I think I shall be able to find him quickly.'

He left and at first she obeyed the terse order. She made no move to leave the study because it seemed that here where Ramón had been there was a sort of comfort and hope. His strength was still here in this room and at the moment she needed that strength badly.

The window was open and she looked out, leaning against the sill and going over in her mind how long it had been since Manuel had left the breakfast-room, how long it had taken to write that note. He could not be too far and Ramón should find him soon—unless he had taken a horse! Sure that his thought would also have occurred to Ramón she stayed where she was for a second but the need to take some action, the growing fear as Ramón failed to come back and the certainty in her own mind that Manuel had been hurt beyond healing by his realisation of her enmity with Ramón, finally drove Meriel to the open front door.

There was not a servant in sight and she knew that they too would have been sent to search for Manuel. She was the only inactive person here and it seemed to have been her fault all the time. There had been no need to shout and rave at Ramón. If he had not meant so much to her, her amusement would have been enough, but she would never be able to treat him in any way other than with deep emotion. She had brought all this upon herself and she was standing here useless.

From across the *llanos* came a sound that had never failed

to raise the hairs on the back of her neck since she had heard it as a child and Ramón had explained what it was to strengthen his warning to her. She listened and sure enough it came again, the loud wailing cry of the jaguar—*el tigre*. It sounded like the call of some monstrous domestic cat but all the words of warning that Ramón had drummed into her came readily to her mind. She had never in all her time here seen *el tigre*, for the killer of the *llanos* took great care to avoid risks. For its size, the most powerful beast of prey in existence, it moved silently in the trees, dropping on its quarry after quiet deadly stalking.

The river! Out on the open savanna there was no place to hide. She remembered how easily Ramón had seen her so long ago when she too was a child. If Manuel had taken a horse he would know well that either Ramón or one of the *llaneros*, the skilled horsemen who worked on the rancho, would track him and outride him easily. But the river gave cover. It twisted and turned for miles, the trees a hiding place for more than a young child. She was suddenly quite certain that this was what Manuel had done and she raced down the steps at the front of the house towards the car she knew would be parked at the side.

It was there, dusty and dented and strangely comforting in its familiarity. With no thought but Manuel she jumped in and found the keys where they were always left, in the glove compartment. It started at once, noisy, dirty but utterly reliable, and for once she blessed Ramón's determination to keep everything as he wanted it. With this car the river was close, the tracks to it easy to see having been worn into the grasses over countless years by the steady trekking of the cattle.

She pulled out of the yard recognising her own state of nerves when she narrowly missed the gate-post, hearing the faint shout that came to her above the noise of the engine but too intent on her mission to pay any heed to it. She pulled off the main road that led to the nearby town and took to the rough track within a few yards and then it took all her concentration to keep the car straight on the bouncing rutted road. She had always somehow had in her mind the picture of these grasslands as they had looked to her as a child. Even though she had ridden here with Ramón, had seen the men moving the herds and watched with delight their skill and beauty in the saddle, still to her the river was as it had been on that day so long ago when she had learned of the existence of *el tigre*.

The river was a place out of bounds, a life-force for the grasslands but a place of terror. This much Ramón had instilled in her and it remained even now. She knew too why the men of the *llanos* referred to the jaguar as if there were only one—*el tigre*—as if it were one overpowering all-knowing creature that never died. It struck terror into all and though they would hunt it if it took cattle they were rarely successful and took their own lives into their hands when they faced the cunning and silence of the cat of the *llanos*.

It was in front of her almost before she realised it, the wide river-bed, almost dry now but with a depth of bank and a width that said only too readily that floods would race through the length of it before too long. For a few yards she drove slowly along the bank-side but it was a hopeless task in the car. Manuel was not likely to come out and greet her if his intention was to hide, and keeping her eye on the rutted edge where the car ran dangerously close to the sheer fall into the river-bed while looking anxiously between the trees was an impossible task. She would never find him this way.

She stopped the engine and sat for a minute listening but there was no sound to tell her that anyone was there other than herself. There was the humming of insects, the faint sound of running water and the vast silence of the plains. She got out and stood by the car, her ears attuned to any sound that might be Manuel, searching with narrowed eyes along the stretch of the river close by. It was impossible to be sure whether anyone was here or not and she knew that if he chose to remain silent she would never find him.

'Manolito!' She shouted only once because the sound of

her own voice into the silence was somehow shocking and frightening, and though she told herself that this was merely a river like any other, she knew perfectly well that it was not. Even so, she walked quietly along the bank, hoping that Manuel could see her and that he would come from his hiding-place and race towards her; but it became clear after a while that he was not about to do anything of the sort and she knew too that he might be at any place along the nearer length of the river. It would take a search party to find him, and coming here alone was a foolishness that Ramón would no doubt point out to her.

With a sigh she began to retrace her steps, thankful that the car was close by, the stillness beginning to oppress her, and then she heard a sound. It was faint, almost as if a hiding person had inadvertently moved and made an unexpected sound of annoyance. It was a mixture between a low grunt of exasperation and a sigh. She stopped, a few feet from the car, and looked around, listening hard, but what she saw was not her brother's face, not his dark pleading eyes. She looked up into the trees and saw the thing she had never seen, the rich reddish-yellow fur, marked with black rosettes, the long watchful eyes half closed and the ferocious mouth opened in a soundless snarl as the great fear of her childhood confronted her, *el tigre*, the killer of the plains, watching her with souless eyes, his body lying so deceptively indolent along a branch, his thick tail hanging down, the end twitching slowly.

Meriel knew that any movement would be the last movement she would ever be able to make. From the corner of her eye she could see the car, so near but unattainable. To stand as she stood now, frozen into immobility, was not likely to preserve her safety for very long but she knew that to run to the car would be the end of her. Silently she prayed, shocked to realise that her prayers were not to some unseen Creator but to Ramón. He would never know how she loved him, and though he would be sorry, his life would go on. Manolito would be shocked beyond recovery by this and she had brought it all on by her inability to obey

Ramón. She was mesmerised by the evil in the eyes of the hunting animal, knowing that even were he to turn now and run away across the river she would be still unable to move. He would not wait indefinitely.

The shot when it came added to her fear and the noise of the galloping horses hardly entered her mind. She saw the huge cat leap, turn and spring to the ground but it was not towards her that he raced, it was to the shelter of the overhanging bank and the safety of the trees across the river. She stood as she had been, paralysed with fear, and even the sound of Ramón's voice, the sight of the men with him as they plunged their horses down the bank in pursuit of the killer failed to bring her back into the present.

'Meriel!' The urgency in Ramón's voice caught her attention and she turned dazed eyes on him, his name soundlessly on her lips as she fell to the baked earth at his feet.

When she came round the car was in motion, Ramón at the wheel, his other arm supporting her as she lay against him. Odd disjointed thoughts flashed through her mind: he had left his horse, he had brought a gun, he had found her. She only realised that she had been murmuring her thoughts aloud when he answered her.

'The men will bring my horse back. I do not suppose that they will get the jaguar but perhaps they will. I knew that I could not hit him, the distance was too great. My only hope was to scare him into flight. I could not reach you in time. He might have attacked long before we got close enough.'

'Ramón! I'm sorry—sorry!' She felt the first healing wave of tears and he pulled her close, resting his head for one moment against hers.

'Never mind. You are safe. We will discuss your latest crime when you are feeling better. For now you are here and safe. Hush, Meriel.'

He sounded deeply moved and she wept silently against him until the storm of tears had passed, still unable to sit up of her own accord.

'Manuel!'

'He is at the *hacienda*!' For the first time, anger entered his voice. 'He was never anywhere else. He has more sense than to cross the *llanos* and head for the river alone; such hot-headed acts he leaves to his sister. *Por Diós*, if the cupboard were still unshelved I would be tempted to take your mother's course of action with the boy. His prank has almost cost you your life.'

'I'm sure he didn't mean it! He had no idea that I would do anything so stupid!'

'No.' He pulled her tightly to his side and sighed despairingly. 'Only I, it seems, know your ability to react foolishly and wilfully. You have frightened yourself badly and you have added several grey hairs to my head. Do not act again without consulting me. I have your promise, Meriel?'

'Yes.' It was a promise that would be easy to keep because she would be going away, away from the plains, away from Venezuela and she would never again know the comfort and peace of Ramón's arms. She let tears flood over her again, but this time it was not fear that brought them to her face, it was love that was as hopeless now as it had ever been.

CHAPTER SIX

STILL unable to stand without support, Meriel was half carried into the *hacienda* and straight to the study when they returned. Manuel was there, sitting bolt upright on the edge of a chair as if he had been told to sit there and not move a muscle.

At the sight of Meriel, his pale face lit up with relief, and he stood to run to her but Ramón's sharp command stopped him instantly.

'Remain in your seat!'

Manuel sank back to his former position, his face growing more pale as he saw the condition of Meriel and Ramón's anger.

'You will spend the time here in observing the shock and distress on the face of your sister!' Ramón said sternly. 'Your foolish prank has almost cost her her life. Henceforth you will remember that when you state an intention it must be truthful!' It was plain to see that he was furious and Manuel did not answer, his eyes were on Meriel's face, on the grazes that her fall to the hard earth of the river bank had produced and on the trembling of her hands.

'She believed your note and acted out of love for you!' Ramón continued angrily as he strode to the cabinet and poured brandy into a glass, taking it back to the settee where he had placed Meriel and holding it to her lips. 'While you were hiding in comfort, Meriel was facing *el tigre!*'

'Merry!' Manuel jumped up in spite of Ramón's angry eyes and ran to his sister, kneeling and burying his face in her lap. 'I'll never do anything like that again. I wanted you to stay, to be friends with Ramón. I did not think . . .'

'It's all right.' She stroked his dark hair with trembling

98

hands. 'Just don't ever do anything like that again. I was so frightened for you.'

'You may now go to your room and you will have the goodness to remain there!' Ramón intervened in a hard voice. 'I wanted you to see her and I wanted you to realise that we are all responsible for our actions. Fortunately, you have not been called upon to live with the idea that your selfishness was the cause of your sister's death.'

Manuel went out with no further word and Meriel looked at Ramón helplessly.

'You think that I am hard?' he asked. 'He has a life of great responsibility before him. Unfortunately neither he nor I can afford the luxury of thinking solely of ourselves.'

'He's only a boy, Ramón,' she said quietly and he nodded in agreement, coming to sit by her and help her to more brandy.

'I know it. He will however have to face some of the life that I have faced even though I wish it were not so. He cannot learn soon enough that the duty he owes to those who care about him is the greatest duty that he has.'

She was silent. She could only agree after all. Even though she was not in any way related, Ramón had faithfully carried out any duty that was necessary as far as she was concerned. It was not his fault that she loved him and she was suddenly filled with a great affection that ran side by side with her love.

'We are both quite a trial to you,' she whispered shakily, managing a smile when he looked at her quickly and questioningly. 'And it's quite funny really, neither of us means to be a trial at all.' She couldn't help the look on her face nor could she stop the hand that came up to touch his face with the timidity and wonder that had been there when she had daringly touched him as a child.

'There are some crosses that I bear gladly,' he murmured with a faint answering smile. 'They say too that lightning does not strike twice in the same place so perhaps your brush with death at the river is a chapter that can be written off.'

He looked deeply into her eyes for a moment and then took her hand as it lay against his bronzed face and turned it to his lips.

'You must now go to bed for a while. I will call Rosita to help you. For myself, I think that it would be a good idea to finish the bottle of brandy and drown my shocks for the rest of the day. However,' he continued, standing and helping her to her feet, 'I have too much to do so I will try to regain my temper and my ease of mind by working.'

He rang the bell and then helped her to the door as they heard the quick steps of Rosita on the passage and her sharp tap on the door of the study.

'Try to sleep,' he advised. 'By dinner time you will be much better.'

She was helped to her room by Rosita who clucked and shook her head impatiently at the antics of her favourites, helping Meriel into bed in her slip when she had bathed the grazes, and within minutes Meriel drifted into sleep, the feel of Ramón's lips still on her hand, his words still in her mind.

It was mid-afternoon when she woke to the slight sound of someone in her room and opening her eyes saw Manuel sitting anxiously on the bed close to her.

'I did not mean to wake you, Merry,' he said softly. 'I wanted to see that you were still all right.'

'Of course I am.' She reached out and ruffled his hair. 'Try to forget all about it now. As it turned out, nothing happened except that I got an awful fright. At least I can now say that I've seen *el tigre*. I expect I'll be proud of that when I get over the fright.'

'Ramón will never forgive me,' Manuel confided with mournful eyes, his expression filled with drama, and she laughed, amusement wiping out the lingering fears.

'Of course he will. It's all over and you get on very well

with him. It's just that we are a big responsibility to him.'

'I think you would not be so sure of his forgiveness if you had seen him,' he said worriedly. 'We saw you drive out of the gate. He had already found me.'

'Where exactly were you?' she asked intrigued by his unexpectedly boyish antics.

'I was in José's small house. He is my friend and I have often hidden there before when Ramón has been—after me.'

'Ah, so you are not as good as I imagined?' she asked her amusement growing. 'He's been after you before then?'

'Yes, I do things wrong, from time to time,' he confessed seriously, 'but this is the greatest thing I have done and when he saw you leave he seemed to know where you were going. He went mad I think and I was glad to go and sit in the study and not move as he had ordered. If he had not found you, he would have killed me.'

'What a very dramatic person you are,' she laughed. 'I'm perfectly sure that Ramón would not have killed you.'

'Do not bank on it!' Ramón's voice from the doorway made them both jump guiltily. 'The thought is even now crossing my mind. You are living very dangerously to disobey me yet again, Manuel!'

He stood there with a forbidding frown on his face, a tray in his hand that was clearly for Meriel, and further words were not needed. Manuel crossed the floor with very hasty steps and in a moment they heard the door of his room close behind him.

'He was only anxious about me,' Meriel began in a placating tone but he looked at her with exasperation as he crossed to the bed and sat beside her, placing the tray on the bedside table.

'He really is very skilled at making his own excuses, he has had many chances to practise,' he said wryly. 'Believe me, he can think up excuses that would never enter your head. I would leave him to cover his own tracks if I were you. I have brought you a little soup,' he added. 'Sit up and take it now.'

'Thank you. I—I'll have it in a minute.' She was in her slip and not about to sit up while Ramón was here.

He raised his dark brows in further exasperation and simply leaned across, placing his hands under her arms and hauled her up in bed, plumping the pillows up behind her and placing the tray firmly on her lap.

'Now!' he ordered sternly. 'I will talk to you as you take the soup and we will have no nonsense.' He wasn't looking at her with any other expression but a determination to get down to business and after a few seconds she quite forgot that apart from the thin ribbon of the straps her shoulders were bare and that the lacy top of her slip was cut véry low, was provocatively scanty.

'You cannot now simply go tomorrow,' he said without preamble, holding up his hand for silence when she would have spoken. 'I am not about to say that Manuel will collapse should you go so soon,' he added, 'it is perhaps dawning on you that he is not quite the defenceless angel that you were at his age. He is an Ortiga. The same blood runs in his veins as runs in my own and the last thing we are is defenceless. I was thinking only of you. You are in no fit state to fly to Caracas, let alone to London. You will therefore stay longer!'

'You don't realise, I suppose, how very domineering you are,' she offered softly, her eyes downcast on the tray, not at all sure how to take this firm decision. She wanted to stay with him but the idea was a dangerous one and she knew that all too well. Better to be thousands of miles away from him. Even now her breathing was difficult and it had nothing to do with the shock of this morning.

'Of course I realise it!' he answered arrogantly. 'I can never see the need to be other than what I am.'

Stunned by his attitude, she raised wide, surprised eyes to his face and found him watching her in amusement. He took the tray and placed it back on the table, his lips twisting at her expression.

'You think that, like your brother, I should make excuses for my conduct! I cannot. Excuses do not sit well on my tongue and I am always sure that I know best.'

'Why, you . . .!' She was open mouthed at his words and he laughed delightedly, a long, low chuckle of pleasure.

'I can ask for forgiveness though,' he confided, his dark eyes warm on her face. 'I am sorry that I could not resist the chance to wind you up into one of your small tempers. I find it fascinating to watch your eyes change from silver to dark grey, to see them grow in your face to keep pace with your anger. It is a pleasure to watch—always provided that you finally give in. I like to win.'

'Now look, Ramón!' she began heatedly, no longer feeling weak either from her fright or his nearness.

'I am looking,' he confessed slowly. 'I have been looking for the past ten minutes and I could remain here and look for days and days.'

His dark eyes moved over her creamy shoulders, her slender neck where a pulse beat frantically in time to the rhythm of her heart, over the beautiful mounds of her breasts where the lacy top only added to the temptation.

'Still you wear the opal,' he commented softly.

'I forgot to—to . . .'

He shook his head, his eyes claiming hers, a fire beginning in their secret depths.

'You forgot nothing,' he murmured, his gaze moving to the deep hollow where the stone lay and then back to her face. 'You still feel my touch on your skin and the opal is warm, a reminder.' His eyes began to move over her features, no longer smiling in their teasing way but possessive and burning, and Meriel sat as still as a mouse, as hypnotised by those gleaming eyes as she had been all her life.

'Once before,' he continued in a low voice, 'I touched you but then it was in the moonlight and you were beautiful, gentle and utterly willing, as you are now.'

She wanted to tell him that she was not, that she was no longer eighteen and vulnerable, but her tongue cleaved to the roof of her mouth, her lips were dry and speech was beyond her. He had come into her room in his usual businesslike way and now he was a different person, sensuous and arousing, his eyes compelling, his whole demeanour dominating her mind. She wetted her lips with the end of her tongue and his eyes followed the movement hungrily, his finger-tip moving to trace the same path along her lip.

'Ramón! I—I . . .'

'Shh!' His hands began to explore her features like a blind man, tracing her cheeks, the smooth curve of her forehead, the delicate line of her chin and the slender length of her neck. There was a strange half-smile on his lips as his eyes followed the slow, seductive movements and saw the quickening rise and fall of her breasts.

He lifted the opal as he had done before, holding it in one hand as his other hand smoothed her shoulder, moving beneath the ribbon of her strap to case it away, but this time he did not let the precious stone fall back into place, he put it there between the mounds of her breasts with slow and deliberate movement, his fingers lingering on the warmth of her skin before opening to spread out across the curve of her breast and claim it possessively.

'No! Ramón!' She gasped out the words but his hand stayed in warm, tender possession as his eyes rose to hers.

'Why do you say no, when you mean yes!' he asked softly. 'Your skin melts to my touch, your eyes offer me everything that I could ever want. Now, I simply want to touch you, to look at you, to know that you are here, warm and willing beneath my hands and not lying dead and violated beside the river.'

His hands moved to slide away the lacy top, letting the ribbons fall down the smooth skin of her arms, and his eyes moved over her as she sat spellbound, unable to stop him as he gazed at her breasts.

'Do you know what I thought this morning when I saw you so still and terrifed, your eyes on the jaguar?' he asked deeply. 'Even before I saw him, I knew the reason for your stillness and fear and terror shot through me too. I thought, she will die. That beautiful face will be lifeless, that slender body knocked to the dust by a killer's stroke, and I have never owned her, never seen her beauty lying naked in my arms, never wakened to the sight of her head on my pillow. You and I,' he continued thickly, 'have been destined to be lovers for more years than I care to remember. You are ready for me and I want you, I will not allow you to leave.'

'I—I won't stay here and become—become ...' The words would not leave her lips and it was useless to deny his words, she wanted him with a deep, lonely longing that had simply grown with the passing of time.

'Become what?' he murmured, his lips trailing arousingly across the tips of her breasts. 'My mistress?' He lifted his head and looked at her with a strange twisted smile. 'You think that I would ask you? You think that is what I intend?'

He lifted her up towards him, his fingers laced in her hair, his eyes burning with desire.

'You imagine that I need a bedmate only, some pliant toy in my hands?' he smiled, his old arrogance flaring. 'If I did, you would come to me, but that is not what I want from you. You have told me so very often that you are an outsider, that you are merely tolerated in this house, in this land. You will be an outsider no longer if that is what you are sure you have been. Your name will be Ortiga, my name. You will be the mother of my children, the one who stands beside me securely when we are beset by my— abominable relatives.' His smile deepened as he reminded her of her own words. 'You are to be my wife. I do not intend to sit here and wait until you have married this— this Englishman or whatever he is. You belong to me and I am claiming you.'

For a second she stared at him, stunned and light-headed.

Whatever she had expected him to say it had never been this. Such hopes and dreams had left her when he had told her to go almost seven years ago. The manner of his speech too frightened her. He had not asked her to marry him, not declared any love for her. He had stated his desire and his intentions and she was expected to obey. A cold shiver ran over her and he pulled her closely to him.

'You are cold, *pequeña*?' he asked softly. 'Your skin burns and your cheeks are pink as a rose. Say that you agree and I will leave you to rest comfortably.

'I—I don't agree,' she got out faintly. 'Stewart wants to marry me because he loves me. You—you don't. You're cold-blooded and . . .'

'Am I?' he whispered into her hair. 'You think he wants you as much as I do? Whatever words he uses to cloak his desire, there is not that between you that is between you and me, or you would not be still as innocent as I know you are.'

'You don't know that I—that we . . .' she began, trying to pull away, but he held her tightly, only allowing her to ease away so that he could see her face.

'You have slept with him?' he asked, only amusement in his eyes.

'No! No—but—but . . .'

'And yet,' he assured her softly, 'were I to lock the door and hold you against me, you would not resist me any more than you would have resisted when you were eighteen and locked in my arms in the moonlight. You have moved from anger to games and to defiance since you have returned, but through it all your eyes have offered me all that I want.'

'I—I won't marry you. It's unthinkable! You're doing this because . . .'

'Because I want you and I intend to have you and I will wait no longer!' he stated with a growing annoyance at her hedging that she could see beginning to darken his face.

He sat her up like an unresisting doll and pulled her straps into place, covering her and then looking at her with determined eyes.

'Enough of this nonsense. You will marry me as soon as I can arrange it and the matter is settled!' He stood and looked down at her, his expression suddenly softening at her wide-eyed fear. 'Tell me, Meriel,' he asked quietly. 'Have you ever suffered hurt at my hands? Does marriage to me frighten you so much that you would refuse to be what you know you long to be?'

'I don't want to be . . .' she began but he tilted her face arrogantly and looked at her with raised brows.

'Lies sit very uneasily on your lips, Meriel,' he stated. 'Even though your lips say one thing, your eyes say entirely the opposite and I am an expert at reading the need in those grey eyes, I have never in my life been told outright by you what your needs were, always I have had to find out the hard way. We will say that the matter is settled.'

He walked out, giving her no chance to speak even if she had been capable of speech. She was dazed, frightened and unable even to think with any clarity. She had imagined this so long ago on that moonlit night, imagined herself the wife of Ramón Ortiga, loved, needed and necessary to his life. Now, within a few minutes, he had announced that she was to be what she had so longed for, but it was too late now, her dreams had been too shattered, her trust almost completely destroyed, and she would always fear him, not physically but with the fear of someone who is never certain of her place in the heart of one she loves. He did not love her, except some lingering affection from the past. Better perhaps to marry Stewart and be a good and affectionate wife, without the enchantment of Ramón's arms, but safe. She knew that she could do neither. She had put off her answers to Stewart for so long and now she knew why.

She dared not stir from her room and it was only the anxiety on Rosita's face that made her change at last for dinner and go down to face Ramón's dark eyes. She was glad to find that Manuel was there already, clearly having been pardoned and allowed to leave the restrictions of his room.

'You look very pale, Merry,' Manuel said worriedly. 'I do hope that you'll stay a little longer now. I—I mean,' he added as Ramón shot him a look of annoyance, 'you don't seem to me to be fit to go so far, well, not yet.'

'Your concern does you credit,' Ramón said drily, 'however, she is not going at all, so calm your fears.'

'Ramón!' Meriel's sharp cry brought both their eyes to her and Manuel looked greatly downcast.

'Please! I didn't mean to bring on another quarrel, I only meant . . .'

'You have brought on no quarrel whatever,' Ramón assured him, giving him a quick smile. 'It is just that Meriel had not perhaps wanted to tell you yet that she is staying, therefore, I will not tell you anything else.' He looked around the table and then at Manuel. 'Would you go and ask Rosita for more butter?'

'Certainly!' Manuel left the table with great alacrity, glad to have escaped for a moment, and Ramón turned at once to Meriel.

'I have telephoned London,' he said evenly as soon as the door had closed behind Manuel. 'I spoke to Mackensie and I have told him that you have resigned. You can confirm it in writing.'

At any other time, she would have flown into a temper, stormed from the room, but now, she felt only regret and an unhappy acceptance that there could be no future here for her without Ramón's love. She sighed, more tired than angry.'

'Oh, Ramón,' she looked at him miserably. 'Why are you doing this? You know that he will ring me and that I'll say entirely the opposite thing. I will not stay here. I'm surprised that he hasn't rang back already.'

'He has.' Ramón sat back in his chair, smiling at her as if she had in fact just agreed to marry him. He was not taking any notice of her wishes or of her refusal. 'He rang almost at once and I was able to tell him that you were not well and asleep.'

'I wasn't!'

'You were,' he assured her firmly. 'I rang the moment that you were safely in your bed and you were certainly asleep when he returned the call. By the time I brought your soup the whole thing was over. One look at you this morning when the jaguar so nearly killed you was quite enough to convince me that this nonsense had gone far enough.'

'You know that I'll ring him and tell him that it's not true. You can't go on pretending that I'm ill.'

'Ring now,' he suggested, still sitting back and watching her with a smile. 'I intend to marry you, not to keep you prisoner. The telephone is yours to use.'

She would have done, except that she felt so tired and except for the fact that Manuel returned at that moment, but more because they all heard against the window and the roof the first drops of rain that heralded the wet season, drops that grew in speed and sound until the rain was thundering against the roof like a thousand drums.

With it too came the first distant roll of thunder and Meriel stiffened in her chair, her eyes anxiously on the windows and the darkening sky.

'The rains are here!' Manuel actually sounded excited and happy, turning to her with glowing eyes. 'There will be a storm, I think.'

'It is too early in the season,' Ramón said quickly, his eyes on Meriel, and subtle though he was, Manuel was not deceived.

'You are afraid of the storms, Merry?' he asked in astonishment. 'I love them, they are so splendid, so noisy, so wild!'

'That, I think, will be enough,' Ramón said quietly, getting to his feet and drawing the curtains as Meriel's scared eyes refused to be sensible and look away. 'And yes, Meriel is afraid of storms. She is not however,' he added quietly, 'afraid of *el tigre* when her brother is in danger, so do not take to yourself any superior attitude.'

'I would not!' Manuel protested. 'Not with Merry. In any case,' he added with a wide grin, 'she is more than a match for me when I am being too big for my boots, that is the expression, is it not, Merry?' he added seriously.

'It will do nicely. It often fits the bill nowadays!' Meriel said wryly.

'I do not understand "fits the bill" either,' Manuel started, but Ramón intervened.

'You understand bedtime, I assume?' he asked softly. 'And that being the case finish your meal and be on your way.'

Knowing full well that Ramón's statement that it was too early in the season for storms had been designed only to calm her, Meriel too went straight to her room after the meal. The thought of telephoning to England had completely left her head and she later stood in her room peering from behind closed curtains into the night. These storms had always frightened her; in fact frightened was perhaps an understatement. They swept down from the high mountains and lashed across the dry plains with a wild ferocity, grand and splendid but terrifying to her. Before them came the rain, torrential and unrelenting as it was falling now, and it was rare indeed to have the force of the rain without the crash of thunder and the searing forks of lightning after the long dry season. Always she had been afraid but tonight her nerves were at breaking-point and she got into bed, thankful that the first signal roll of thunder had not yet brought the storm. The rain fell in torrents but that was not the noise she feared and finally she fell asleep, worn out by the most shattering day of her life, still keeping her ears attuned for the danger of the storm, her mind refusing to think about Ramón's plan for her life.

Next morning the whole thing had receded to a dream-like

quality, and Meriel went to breakfast with the certainty that she would be able to sort things out very soon. She was unprepared for the sight of Ramón, still lounging at the table, any work that he had to do being ignored.

'I imagined that you would be out by now,' she murmured as he held her chair courteously. 'Isn't Manuel here!'

'Not yet,' he answered easily, resuming his seat and leaning back to watch her with veiled amusement and the faint ghost of teasing at the back of his eyes. 'We have a few minutes alone. Eat your breakfast and then I have something to show you.'

'What?' she asked with growing anxiety. Now that she was sitting here opposite him, her confidence was not nearly so strong, especially when he kept looking at her like that with narrowed amused eyes.

'Later, do not be impatient,' he advised, adding, almost as an afterthought, 'You have telephoned to England?'

'No. You know I haven't!'

'Ah, yes, the *tormenta*! It did not arrive after all, did it? I waited to see if you would have need to be terrified but in the event there was rain only. Perhaps it will come in late this year.'

'Good? Let it wait a few days and then I'll not be here. I'll be back in England where storms are more reasonable.'

To her consternation, he laughed delightedly and leaned across to capture her hand.

'If you wish to play hard to get, do so,' he offered softly. 'I will go ahead with the marriage arrangements secretly if you wish and then I can always propose to you again, suddenly, perhaps in the moonlight.'

'You didn't propose to me!' she snapped, blushing furiously. 'You—you stated your intentions and never asked mine. There's no way that you can make me . . .'

'I can make you do anything that I want, be anything that I want, and we both know that,' he said softly, his thumb probing her palm erotically. 'Why not make your call to England now?'

He was challenging her to try to escape him and she rose to the bait.

'I will!' She strode into the hall angrily and made the call. Stewart was not there. He was not at his flat either and she replaced the receiver slowly, looking up to see Ramón leaning against the door, his arms folded, his eyebrows quizzical.

'No reply? He is not then shattered by your resignation, this man of great virtue? Perhaps he has some other nice girl lined up for your job after all. It is as well, he cannot have you.'

She turned abruptly away but he caught her wrist and pulled her towards him.

'Come here,' he said softly. 'I promise not to tease you again for the whole of the day no matter how much you tempt me. Come, your breakfast can wait. I want to show you something outside.'

With no alternative, she went. He was not about to release her hand and she was not up to any struggle so she stepped into the cool garden and walked in a worried silence beside him, her hand tightly in his.

'Cheer up,' he said softly. 'I have not captured *el tigre* and kept him in the stables to spring out at you. I wanted only to show you something that you have apparently forgotten. Your black foal,' he added when she looked at him in surprise. 'You have not asked about him since you returned home.'

'I—I never thought. I only saw him for such a brief time.' She felt guilty for no good reason and her annoyance showed on her face.

'You are in a very bad mood today,' he commented. 'Perhaps I can change that.'

They came to the paddock and her eyes widened at the sight of the foal, identical to the one she had seen so long ago, to all intents and purposes the same.

'No,' he laughed as she looked up in astonishment. 'I have

not discovered a way to stop things ageing. This is another one. Your original one is now a very mature stallion and this is a foal he sired. This time you will see him grow, and this time I will see you ride him. This time to, we shall have a naming ceremony.'

She walked to the fence and saw the foal turn and quickly move towards them.

'You still tempt them with your sugar?' she asked, annoyed at the warmth that flooded over her as she remembered the night she had seen Ramón's method of bringing the animal to him.

'Yes.' He was suddenly quiet and serious-faced. 'I have something for you too and it is not sugar.' Before she could protest, she was moved to the fence, her back against it as Ramón stood close to her making movement away impossible. For a moment he looked at her and then his hand stroked down her face.

'While you were shopping in Caracas,' he said softly, watching her, 'I too went to the shops.' He felt in his pocket and took out a small black velvet-covered box. 'Give me your hand, Meriel,' he ordered softly. 'It is time that you carried the proof of our future on your finger for all to see.'

She was so stunned that she never resisted and he slid the ring, a large glittering diamond, on to her finger.

'Ramón!' She suddenly came to life, but her protests died in her throat as he looked at her and pulled her towards him, his gaze heated enough to burn her, his hands hard and demanding.

'Refuse me and I think I shall kill you!' he said in a deep whisper. 'I shall never allow another to take you.'

His lips covered hers as he pressed her against the fence, the weight of his powerful body holding her prisoner as his hands moved over the softness of her body.

'You know with a certainty that you cannot deny that you are mine,' he breathed, his mouth coming down to cut off any protests, opening over hers and making her tremble in a kiss that was like possession, all-consuming, his tongue plundering her mouth, his hands moulding her to him.

'You wear my ring, you are mine,' he said against her hair after a while, holding her trembling body close. 'From today, everyone will know and soon we shall be married.'

He lifted his head and looked down at her, his hand tilting her chin and he simply waited, saying nothing, watching her until his eyes seemed to be the only thing in the world as she felt herself sink towards him, drowning in his gaze.

'Yes.' She hardly recognised the whisper as her own, was hardly aware that with that one word she had committed her future into the hands that caressed her now, powerful hands that thrilled and frightened her. He was danger and comfort, cruelty and compassion, all she longed for and all she feared. He did not love her but she could never go away. She melted towards him and he kissed her eyes closed with tenderness.

'I have taught you the meaning of a promise, my elusive little sweet,' he murmured. 'This is a promise that you will never be released from. You have given me that answer I wanted and now you are mine.'

For a few seconds, she felt the full power of his passion and then he released her with reluctance, his breathing harsh and uneven.

'I think that here is not the place to let you know my feelings,' he said ruefully. 'Come back to the house and finish your breakfast. We shall name the horse another day.'

He turned her to the house and she was glad of the arm that he kept tightly around her. Queer bursts of feeling were warring inside her. Fear at what she had promised, excitement at his nearness and what his eyes had silently told her, and an uneasiness about the future that she thrust to the back of her mind.

She raised her eyes as they came to the house and the past was relived in a few horrified seconds. On the step stood Doña Barbara and beside her, as before, Carmen and

Consuelo Sandoval. She stiffened, but this time Ramón's arm tightened, his hand moving over her hip and splaying possessively against her stomach in an embrace that suggested an intimacy that was not in any way the affection of a man for his stepsister. As they moved forward, his hand also moved to her nape, soothingly and warmly caressing her openly before the horrified gaze of his aunt.

'An unexpected but timely visit, Tia Barbara,' he said with a beaming smile. 'You have saved me a great deal of trouble. Now I can tell you in person what I would have had to travel many miles to say. Meriel is home, as no doubt Carmen told you, and this time she will not leave us again. She is to be my wife and we shall marry as soon as the ceremony can be arranged. I have waited too long for her to take any delays with patience. You may put your mind to it and help me out. The ceremony at the *hacienda*, do you think?'

What she thought was all too clear. She turned on her heel and went inside, a white-faced Carmen escorting her, and Consuelo Sandoval was left to face them alone.

'They are overcome,' Ramón said with caustic humour. 'At this moment, no doubt, Tia Barbara will be thinking that our children will be brilliantly blonde and that the end of the world is near. You will offer your congratulations, Consuelo. We are stunned at the effect we have had on my aunt, are we not, my love?'

Meriel found that she too was simply staring at him, no doubt as white-faced as the other women, but he smiled into her eyes and kissed her lips lightly.

'We will congratulate ourselves then.'

'I'm sorry, Ramón.' Recovering quickly, Consuelo moved forward and Meriel steeled herself to hear words that she knew would come out now. At eighteen she had been in no doubt of the relationship between Ramón and the beautiful Venezuelan woman. How would she take this announcement that had been thrust upon her without warning? But Consuelo smiled brilliantly, kissing Ramón on the cheek, before turning to embrace Meriel. 'Of course I congratulate you. Meriel is beautiful and the children will be beautiful too, in spite of your aunt's misgivings.'

Meriel acknowledged that this was a masterly performance and she could only admire her. If Ramón had ever announced to her that he was to marry another woman she knew that she would have collapsed, but the congratulations had come readily even though shock had held her fast for a few moments. She was a warm and lovely woman, with kindness of heart that shone from her eyes, even though at the back of those beautiful eyes there was a kind of haunted sadness.

CHAPTER SEVEN

AFTERWARDS Meriel was never sure how she managed to survive the next few hours. Until now it had seemed so unreal, like some bitter-sweet game that Ramón played with her, sensual, exciting, but impossible. A part of her mind had refused to accept the reality of it, knowing that she could never be a permanent part of his life. Now, the stage was being set with a thorough, almost ruthless vigour by Ramón that left no room for doubt. It was announced, the ring was on her finger, she seemed to be surrounded by astonished and disbelieving people and Ramón kept her under his hand like a captive slave.

She recalled wondering how Doña Barbara looked now after almost seven years. It could be summed up in one word—shocked! The imperious face seemed to have aged in minutes and she sat tightly upright in the breakfast-room, apparently having made for the first chair available, her lips in one tight line, white-edged with anger as Carmen stood beside her. They were as forbidding a pair now as they had ever been, starchily dressed in a style that looked more of the last century than this one, formidable enemies.

Only Ramón's power in their lives made them hold their tongues. They were wealthy, she knew that, but they were also completely under Ramón's domination. Their wealth was from shares in the Ortiga empire and Ramón wielded the power there. Chairman and major stockholder, he had never left them in any doubt that they owed their life-style and fortunes to him. The Ortiga inheritance was tied up securely, the shares only theirs for their lifetime. They were not able to sell or bargain and their rights were strictly limited. Only Doña Barbara's age and the deference due to

117

her as his aunt made him consult her at all and she knew better than to cross him although she might be fainting with rage.

'I regret the shock we have given you,' he said silkily as he came into the room with Meriel, Consuelo beside them. 'Had you not arrived so suddenly you would have been informed in a less spectacular manner, but as you are here, I can hardly pretend that nothing is different. Meriel wears my ring and we do not intend to wait for long.'

'I—I'm very happy for you.' The words were choked out, forced from her throat by the necessity for courtesy. 'It was, as you say, a shock. I really should have known. We have all seen the way you have looked after her. At least, she knows our ways and that is suitable.'

There was a veiled condescension in the tight voice that made Meriel stiffen but she knew that she would have to expect this for ever. She was always to be as she had been, a tolerated outsider.

'It would be well, I think, for the family to become accustomed to Meriel's ways,' he said quietly, steel behind the silk. 'She is as firm in her ways as we are in ours and as she is to rule my life from now on, certain adjustments will have to be made. She will be in complete control of the house and no doubt will want to make alterations, and do not forget that her children will be heirs to the Ortiga wealth and fortunes. I think that from now on there will be a slight but noticeable shift of emphasis. Meriel is a little different from all of us, her life has been spent between two continents and she is a great success in her own right. Her new outlook will no doubt ginger us all up and put a little vigour into things.'

There was a silence so deep that Meriel dared not breathe, but her eyes found Manuel's as he sat at the table listening, his eyes as round as the moon. She moved uneasily when he stood and walked across to them, his eyes on her face.

'I think that I do not understand what is happening,

Merry,' he said quietly. 'I think though that you are wearing Ramón's ring and that you are not going away again?'

'She is going to marry me,' Ramón told him with a sudden gentleness in his voice. 'She will not leave us alone and unhappy again. I think that we both have what we want, Manuel.'

'It is all right, to make Merry your wife?' Manuel asked with lingering anxiety.

'She is not my sister, I am happy to say,' Ramón assured him softly. 'I think that it will mean that you now have a greater claim on her, you will have a very complicated relationship and she will be hard pressed to get rid of you.'

'I must say, congratulations.' Manuel stood stiffly and shook hands gravely with Ramón who looked down at him with equal gravity and nodded. Then, with a whoop of delight, Manuel threw his arms around Meriel and hugged her breath away, all boy again and filled with glee.

'You said that you hated him! It was not true. I think it was a lovers' quarrel. But,' he added his face suddenly falling, 'I will not be a pageboy at your wedding! I absolutely refuse to.'

'You are too small to give the bride away,' Ramón said soothingly, 'but I can promise that you will suffer no such indignity as to be a pageboy. You may consider yourself to be an honoured guest. As to the lovers' quarrel,' he added in amusement, 'remind me to check your reading material. You are perhaps though simply seeing too much television.'

For a few moments they had been one small family unit and Meriel had forgotten the existence of the forbidding aunt and cousin. She was reminded though at once.

'Surely such haste is not a good idea,' Doña Barbara began, her colour somewhat restored and with it her confidence. 'It is usual in our family to wait.'

'I have waited,' Ramón informed her sharply, his gaze going to Meriel's face and softening at once. 'I have waited for at least ten years and that is a measure of self-discipline that is an example to any man. One week if it can be arranged, and the wedding here at the *hacienda!*'

After that there was nothing to say, and it was apparent even to his aunt that her services were not really required, her advice not to his liking and therefore dismissed. Meriel ate her breakfast in a hazy dream, wondering when she was going to wake up and realise that it was all untrue, her ears picking up the faint sound of raised voices from the study as Ramón talked to his aunt and her eyes painfully aware of the annoyance on Carmen's face and the utter misery on Consuelo's.

To her credit, the beautiful Venezuelan girl tried to keep some sort of conversation going, but Carmen said nothing at all and Meriel was too dazed to help very much. They were all glad when Ramón announced that he was going to fly them to Caracas after lunch and that he would not return for at least two days.

Now that he had what he wanted, he seemed disposed to get on with his affairs and ignore Meriel, a situation she was well accustomed to in her life here. It took a great deal of courage to enter the study and confront him when she had thought through all the things that would have to be arranged. He seemed to be giving no thought to the wedding now that he had her promise and had made his announcements.

'I want to talk to you,' she began when he called for her to come in. 'There's a lot to discuss and . . .'

'I will try to get back in two days,' he said, continuing to leaf through papers, his mind clearly elsewhere, and her temper soared at such indifference.

'Well, then, shall I discuss my problems with Manolito? As he seems to be the official mouthpiece when you're too preoccupied to answer me, perhaps I should ask him about the wedding-gown, my father, my job and all the other bits and pieces.'

He looked up slowly, simply raising his eyes and surveying her beneath dark brows, his eyes narrowed.

'You do n...
'Your father...
dress will hav...
small but dema...
am not about t...

'Then perhap...
advised him sharp...
fit me into your bu...

She turned to the...
swift strides, closing t...
it, his hands on either s...
her with dark intent ey...

'If you are wanting to...
father, tie up the loose en... ...... the
answer is no!' he bit out. ...... be bought in
Caracas, a few hours away, an... ...e you there as soon
as I come back. We can if you w... have the wedding in two
weeks instead of one so that you may fuss to your heart's
content, but you will not return to England!'

'So I'm a prisoner?' she asked, her temper rising at his
indifference to her feelings for her father. 'I'm to stay here
like a patient child waiting for you?'

'I had hoped that you would stay here waiting for me
with a great deal of impatience,' he said softly, his lips
beginning to brush her forehead gently. He was not
touching her except for this persistent caress but it was
enough to ease all her temper away and she was hard
pressed to remain passively leaning against the old door. 'I
have been impatient for a long time while you lived a
separate life in England. Two days of waiting is surely not
asking too much.'

'I—I only wanted to—to . . .' She made the mistake of
raising her eyes to his and he was smiling down at her with
amusement.

'So do I,' he whispered softly. 'I want to very much
indeed.'

'Ramón!' As colour flared into her face she raised her

THE ORTIGA MARR...

fingers to his lips in an instinct...
that fell so sensuously from...
hand from his mou...
them into pleasura...
deeply pleasure...
through her...
sound, a...
by d...
th...

ve gesture to stop the words
his curved lips and he raised his
king her fingers in his and drawing
n, sucking each one in turn. It was so
ble, so tormenting that physical pain shot
like torture and she gave an odd litle gasp of
whimper of distress, a signal that he acknowledged
awing her into his arms and turning her until he was
e one leaning against the hard warmth of the oaken door.
His fingers tangled in her hair as he drew her unresisting
into the hard demand of his hips, his mouth opening above
hers and taking her lips with urgent demand.

Now that she had promised, now that she wore the ring
there was no resistance in her. She was all melting warmth,
her bones turned to water as they stood locked together in
an embrace that was almost frantic in its enjoyment. His
lips searched hers deeply, his hands tight on her hips as he
held her against the swiftly growing desire of his body. All
her fears fled as if they had never been and there was no
house, no relatives, no past, only the moment and the need
that raced through them both like a fire across the plains.

When he raised his head, his breathing a harsh gasp in
his throat, Meriel clung to him, her open mouth against his
neck, the taste of his skin, salty and heated on her tongue,
years of longing in her movements as she twisted against
him.

'Meriel!' His voice was a shaken plea, deep and violent.
'Dear God! Stop or I will take you now with the house beset
by disapproving faces and the floor hard and unyielding
against your back!'

The hard reality of his words sank in slowly and she
faced his dark glittering eyes with flushed face and dazed
unseeing eyes, still leaning towards him as he lifted her
away from the burning arousal that had fired her own
sexuality.

'We're engaged—we . . .' she began in a trembling
whisper.

'And you have decided to surrender to me now, and here?' he asked, his voice still shaken with desire. 'I had thought that I would have to coax you into submission in spite of the messages of your eyes. I forgot that you are not still my timid little waif of so long ago. You are now a go-getting, fast-talking salesperson.' He was trying to take the tension and the stinging excitement out of the air and she saw the white flash of his smile before she lowered her lashes to hide her growing shame and confusion.

'Now we have the quick slide into the past,' he teased. 'How will I ever discover the real you? Who is in here? Who is really in that lovely head?' He cupped her face and looked with smiling eyes into hers, and her blushes were painful on her face.

'You know,' she quipped shakily, 'a bad-tempered, businesslike . . .'

'Be quiet!' he suddenly ordered. 'We can so readily tease each other into a situation that will be resolved in a few minutes of wild passion right here. When you come to me it will be for much longer than that and I will have you sobbing in my arms for the fulfilment you need. I have waited too long for it to be over in a burst of gratification.' He released her with one stinging kiss on her lips, a groan torn from him when she instantly moved against him. 'We are both hungry,' he said harshly as he strode to his desk, his back taut beneath the shirt that was still damp against his tight muscles. 'It is a hunger that will have to wait for the time and the place. About your worries . . .'

'It doesn't matter,' she said in a soft voice. 'I'll telephone my father and—and then I'll wait.'

He looked across at her, saying nothing, but she was sure that words were not far away, but although she waited, her heart thumping with anxiety, he said nothing and turned his eyes back to the work piled up on his desk. For one brief second she felt that there was a resolution to confess something that was hidden deep in those eyes, but whatever it was, he decided to keep silent and there was nothing she could do about that. She knew him too well.

After the others had gone, the house was suddenly too silent, an air of waiting about the whole place. She knew that by now every servant would know that her new status here was to be as Ramón's wife. They did not need to be told officially, they seemed to have their own secret telegraph that spread like wildfire through the whole estate. Manuel she had expected to question her, to be excited and eager for news, but he was simply quietly happy and her guess was that Ramón had told him to keep out of things for the present. In any case he was to be too busy because later in the morning she heard the sound of a voice she had once known well.

Arturo Morales had once for a very short time in her life been a tutor here for her, and now, with the need for mourning over, he had returned to take up his normal duties with Manolito. She smiled into his surprised and austere face as she went down the corridor to meet him and for a moment his eyes narrowed in thought before his face relaxed into a smile of greeting.

'Señorita Meriel, is it not?' he asked quietly. 'My one-time student and the best loved sister in the world from what I gather from my small and talkative charge.'

'I'm flattered that you remember me, Señor Morales,' she smiled, shaking the hand that had come out to meet hers. 'My stay here was quite short as it turned out.'

'I could not forget such brilliantly shining hair,' he remarked, 'and the colour is not really normal for Venezuela. More than that though I am constantly reminded of your existence by Manuel, who has always been in a fever of excitement when he was to visit you in your country.'

'This is Merry's country now,' Manuel's voice announced with all the determination of his older brother. 'Merry is going to marry Ramón and stay here for ever. When they have children I shall be their uncle, or so Ramón told me. I shall like that,' he added with a smile at

Meriel that had her trying to control the blush that stained her cheeks.

'Well,' Arturo Morales looked long and hard at Meriel and then smiled his usual tight but genuine smile. 'It should have come as no shock to everyone I think? From a child you seemed to be in Ramón's care, it is only natural that he would feel deeply enough to wish to make you his wife. I am very happy for you. Now we will get on with our studies,' he added, turning purposefully to Manuel. 'Sadly much time has been lost.'

She stood there after they had gone and his words ran round her head, chasing each other. There was something so steadily rooted in the past in this place. It was not out of the ordinary to think that there would be a tutor here. There were good schools in Venezuela but it was more in keeping with the place that Manuel should be taught here. It had never been given any consideration when she had asked to go to school when she was a child, and Señor Morales was clever and good at his job. Did her marriage too fit into this comfortable acceptance of the past, that Ramón had treated her as a charge from the first time she had come here and that it was only natural that he should make her his wife?

She remembered his words from this morning when he had spoken to his aunt. 'I have waited for ten years.' Ten years! How old had she been then? Thirteen? Fourteen? Had he looked at her and said to himself that she would do very nicely when she was older? Was she in any way a threat to the inheritance? No. She was not in any way related, a slight tie perhaps through her mother. It was all so unsettling, and the memory of his eyes looking with thoughtful consideration as she had waited earlier for him to speak the words that seemed to be hovering on his tongue came back to her clearly. She knew far less than she should know as his future wife. All she was sure of was her love for him and his undoubted desire for her. She would have to wait and see what the future brought. In the meantime, there was her father.

His silence when she told him that she was about to marry Ramón brought a tremor of unhappiness into her heart. He knew that once again she was going to stay in Venezuela and leave him, and it took considerable effort on his part to control the steadiness of his voice.

'Do you love this stepbrother of yours, Meriel, or have you been brow-beaten into agreeing to marriage?'

'You're very astute, Daddy,' she said tremulously, 'but there's nobody here to bully me and in any case, Ramón wouldn't permit it. We're marrying because we love each other.' A white lie, but she had to believe in it or her world would crumble. He felt strongly enough to want to marry her anyway and she would have to be content with that, she would have to hope.

'Then I'm happy, my dear,' he said quietly. 'I haven't forgotten how Ramón, made your life there bearable and I haven't forgotten too that you so obviously pined for him when you were here at school. I should have expected it, I suppose, but with you being away from him for so long, I had almost forgotten the attachment you used to have towards him.'

'Will you come to see me married?'

'I'll come.' The two words seemed to open all the valves of her tears, all the little fears she had carried in her head for days, all the pent-up emotion about her feelings for Ramón, all the deep misgivings flooded to the surface and eased themselves in tears she could not hide from her father.

'Meriel! Why are you crying? My dearest child, you surely thought that I'd come? Did you expect me to say no?'

'I thought—thought you might not because—I—mean . . .'

'Because of Inez?' His voice was gentle and quiet. 'It was so long ago, Meriel, and I'm sorry she died. After all, she gave me you even if now because she took you out to Venezuela I seem to be losing you.'

'You'll never lose me, Daddy!' Meriel's voice was urgent

and quick even through her tears and she heard his laughter from so many miles away.

'Love is not selfish, Meriel,' he assured her. 'In any case, I win. One day I'll have grandchildren, won't I?'

Yes. Ramón had said that he needed an heir. Once again, the links with the distant past came clearly to her mind. It seemed so cold-blooded. These days people married for love, not to produce an heir, but here, in this house, things seemed sometimes to have advanced very little from the old formalities of days long past.

Her next call was to Stewart and once again, he was not there, not able to be contacted even though they knew perfectly well who was calling. Clearly then nobody knew where he was. Having discovered that she was not going to return, he had simply gone away and made no further attempt to contact her. She felt somehow let down, betrayed. For two years Stewart had been urging her to marry him and now he had simply crossed her off. So many times in her life she had been dismissed and now, here in this house with the painful past around her, it was easy to feel as she had done so many years ago, an outsider of no consequence, lost and alone. She suddenly needed Ramón with a feeling that was akin to desperation. He was something to cling to, had always been her rock and refuge. Even if he was not in love with her as she was with him, there was a sort of love there, she was sure of that, even if it was only an affection. Her lingering doubts about the marriage fled and she would have told him honestly if he had been there at that moment.

Meriel was amused at the subtle change in the attitude of the servants over the next two days. From being an oddity and then an infrequent visitor she had now become in their eyes the mistress of the house. Only Rosita remained the same. The riders too that she saw from time to time as they came into the stables and their quarters that stretched beyond the confines of the gardens of the house greeted her with a new deference, a shy and subdued attitude that was clear in the quick lowering of their bold eyes as they saw her. Señor Ortiga had chosen his bride and henceforth her position was an honoured one.

He phoned during the second day, the only time he had contacted her, and she was careful to show no eagerness as she answered. Her heart was beating like a hammer merely at the sound of his voice and she had to make two attempts to say hello.

'You are all right, Meriel?' he asked quickly. 'There is nothing wrong?'

'No, why should there be? Everything is going along smoothly. Manuel is with his teacher and everyone is going about their normal business.'

'And you? What are you doing?' There was a deep softness in his voice that brought a quick flush to her face and she was glad that nobody could see her.

'Nothing of importance. I've telephoned my father.'

'And?' She felt rather than heard the sudden stillness in him.

'He'll come to the wedding. I'll make arrangements when we know the—the date.'

She heard his quiet laughter, the stiffness leaving his voice as he said, 'Even over the telephone your shyness is apparent. How can you be shy with me? We have known each other for so long, have been friends for most of your life.'

'Were we friends, Ramón?' she asked a little wistfully. 'I don't remember feeling the same about you that I would think one would feel about a friend. You were always so—so cool.'

'Cool? Yes, perhaps, but there has always been much between us, do not attempt to deny that, Meriel. It was a strange destiny that brought you into my life and a great tragedy that forced you to return.'

'If there had been no accident then I would never have come back,' she reminded him quietly. 'I suppose then that

I would never have seen you again. My life was going along a different path.'

'Towards Mackensie!' he stated harshly. 'He has been in touch with you?'

'No. I rang but he's not even in contact with the office, I don't know where he is.' There was a note of anger in his voice when he spoke of Stewart and she wished the conversation had taken a different turn. 'I'd better write and confirm my resignation.'

'Yes. I'll be back either late tonight or in the morning. I have to call first and see the Sandovals.'

'Consuelo?' Her hand gripped the telephone convulsively as she asked and it was impossible to keep the sharp anxiety out of her voice.

'I expect that she will be there, yes. It is however her father that concerns me at the moment.' His voice was edged with laughter again when he continued, 'I am permitted to address a few words to her if she is there? You are not too jealous, *pequeña*?'

'I'm not jealous at all, why should I be? We're marrying because—because it's convenient and sensible. We're not in love. I wouldn't want to clip your wings in any way, Ramón.'

'How very generous and modern,' he murmured with soft derision. 'What a very accommodating partner you are going to be.' He waited for her reply but she said nothing, she couldn't. She had never been able to cope with Ramón as he was now, and loving him so desperately had left her utterly defenceless.

'The Sandovals have a problem,' he told her when it became clear that she would stand there in silence until he spoke again. 'I doubt if I can help but I must at least attempt to help.' There was a changed tone to his voice, a sudden caressing note that held her spellbound. 'You have no cause for jealousy, I want only you. I think that I am probably annoyed that you are not jealous, but again, I know you too well to imagine that you would calmly allow me to go on seeing other women. As I am impatient to get back to you and make sure that you do not fly from me, you may be assured that my visit to the home of Consuelo will be short and businesslike.'

The tone of his voice warmed her for the rest of the day, and even though he did not come that night Meriel went to bed with a sort of blissful contentment flowing through her veins and fell into a deep sleep.

It was after twelve when she awoke with a start to hear the reverberating sound of thunder lingering in the air, knowing that it was some great crash of sound that had awakened her, and she was instantly on guard, her feet out of bed as if prepared for flight although there was nowhere to run to and she knew it.

It came again, a mighty crash of sound that seemed to shake the whole house and then roll around the walls for ages, the lightning filling the whole room. She felt for the lamp switch beside her bed, gasping in fright and beginning to shake when she discoverd that there was no power. It was not unusual, she knew, and though the emergency generator would soon take up the load for the moment she was alone, in the darkness, facing the storm with almost as much fear as she had faced the jaguar, in spite of Ramón's boastful statement on her behalf.

She ran to the window to pull the curtains even closer together and this was the moment that the biggest crash of thunder chose to make itself felt. It seemed to be coming in at the window, seemed to be in the room beside her and she ran for the door, sobbing with fear, straight into arms that grasped her and held her close. A scream bubbled up in her throat but it was never heard because a hand, firm and gentle, came across her mouth, adding to her fear, making her struggle wildly in a mindless panic.

'It's all right. Meriel. I am here. There is nothing to worry about, nothing to be afraid of.' Ramón's voice, deep and reassuring, steadied her and she buried her face in the hard warmth of his shoulder, hiding from the brilliant lightning that seemed to tear through the room.

'I know, I know, but it doesn't help at all. Logic is wasted on me when there's a storm.'

'I know that,' he soothed quietly. 'I also know that to tell you to get into bed and try to sleep is a waste of time.'

She nodded silently, burrowing against him, her eyes tightly shut.

'Manuel!' she asked suddenly, looking up and finding that it was too dark to see his face.

'Asleep. I was just about to check the emergency generator when the biggest crash came. I had already found to my surprise that you were still asleep. I didn't expect you to sleep through that, though. Manuel is not at all like you, he loves the violence of a storm.'

'I wish the lights were on,' she whispered, certain that she had to be quiet in case the sound of her voice drew the storm's ferocity down upon her.

'I will look at the generator,' he whispered back, laughter in his voice. 'You will be safe for a few minutes. Sit on the bed.'

He would have to go to the far end of the house, she knew that, the part furthest away from her, and for the moment she stood exactly as he had left her, but the window drew her like a magnet.

For the moment there was only the sound of the rain and she relaxed a little. Often the storms passed with the same speed as they had arrived, and perhaps now it was going away, rolling back to the mountains.

She peered through the curtains and saw that the night was no longer completely black. The sky was lighter as if the moon was coming to scatter the storm clouds and bring tranquillity. Not yet though. The biggest bolt of lightning she had ever seen shot down to the earth, the thunder crashing at the same time. It seemed to be almost in the garden and this time she screamed, beginning to sob with fear even when Ramón's arms again found her and held her close.

'The generator is not working for some reason,' he said in the sort of matter-of-fact voice he reserved for these occasions. 'Manuel is still asleep and everything is all right. The storm is passing. Look out of the window, Meriel.'

'No!' She clung to him as hard as she could but he persisted, leaning over to open the curtains and turn her to a view of the night sky.

'Look! The clouds are lifting and there is the moon. It is over. The storm has passed.'

'You know it sometimes comes back,' she said, backing close to him, trembling still. 'It often does. It rolls round the mountains and then sweeps back.'

'What does it matter?' he asked softly. 'I am here and I will not leave you.'

'I didn't know you were back,' she whispered. She could see the moon making its way across the night sky, the clouds parting to allow it passage, and the light began to penetrate the room, bathing the area around the window in soft light.

'I decided to fly in late,' he said, his hands warm on her chilled shoulders. 'I just beat the storm. Tomorrow the plane must be moved because soon the lower airstrip will be useless to us. It is time that the cattle were moved higher too. I shall be busy.' His hands were beginning to mould her shoulders, almost absent-mindedly as if he had no real idea that he was caressing her as they both looked out across the moonlit garden, and it was only natural to move closer to him, to feel the warmth of him pressed close to her body.

'Are you cold?' Ramón's voice was almost in her ear as he bent his head to speak. His breath was warm against the side of her face and her skin tingled where the heat of his breath fanned her cheek. 'You are still shivering.' His lips moved to her hair and he rubbed his face against the silken gleam of it, his action tender, making her catch her breath on a small whisper of sound.

'I—I know . . . I'm not cold though, at least, I don't feel it. I'm probably still frightened.'

'The storm is over. What is frightening you now?'

She shook her head, unable to answer, filled with a kind of exhilaration after the passing of her fear, and with the feel of his hands as they slid up her arms to find her shoulders again and urge her to greater contact. A feeling of wild excitement filled her that she had found him here in the darkness, gentle and caring, a deep quiet about him that frightened and thrilled her both at the same time. A slowly growing heat was seeping through every cell of her body and she was so attuned to him that she could almost hear his inner thoughts, could feel the waiting in him, knew that there was a trembling inside him to match her own.

She let all her deepest feminine instincts take her in control, feeling free as she had never before felt in her life, relaxing against him completely, her head resting back against his shoulder.

'Meriel!' He breathed her name against her skin, his lips trailing along her cheek as his hands moved to her hips, holding her tightly, moving her against him with an almost savage, primitive movement, his breath a shuddering sigh against the smooth arch of her neck.

'You are dangerous in the moonlight, you little witch,' he groaned. 'I feel as I felt that night in the moonlight so long ago, ready to devour you, and you were afraid.'

'Yes.' Her whisper trembled from her lips as she softened to his hardness.

'You know what you are doing to me,' he accused thickly, his hands moving with slow caress to the fullness of breasts that surged to the warmth of his palms. 'I have taken care of you, protected you all your life in this house.'

It was a plea for her to move away as if he were incapable of breaking the contact himself, and a surge of feeling shot through her at the power she held over this dark, strong man whose hands trembled with desire.

'You can't protect me from myself,' she whispered, her lips turning to the taut column of his neck, her mouth open as she discovered the heat of his skin.

'And if I cannot resist your temptation? If I do not want

to resist the slender, warm body in my arms, what then, my beautiful Meriel? Tomorrow you will be mine in no uncertain way, tonight I will not leave you unless you send me away. I cannot stay here and touch you. I want more and your chance to send me away aching and empty is fast receding.' He slid his hands from her breasts down the smooth shape of her to the curve of her thighs, his touch strong and demanding, back to her waist and across the warm curve below, pressing her close. 'I want you,' he breathed huskily. 'Send me away.'

She turned in his arms, searching for his lips, wrapping her slim arms around his neck, sliding her fingers into the crisp blackness of his hair, stroking the strength of his tight shoulders beneath the silken white of his shirt, and his control snapped like a wire that has been stretched beyond its limits as he claimed her mouth, covering her lips with small hungry kisses, his breathing a harsh sound in his throat.

Time lost its meaning as they stood locked together, moving like shadows in an erotic moonlit dance, each eager to touch the other, neither of them prepared to move even a fraction of an inch away, a raging need to become fused together that each acknowledged silently holding them in a swaying, moving rhythm of passion.

Meriel shivered as her night-dress slid to the carpet and his arms closed tightly around her again, lifting her lightly against him as he carried her across the moonlit room.

'Let me warm you, my sweet, beautiful Meriel,' he murmured against her lips. 'Let me love you until we are both on fire.'

She clung to him as he placed her on the bed, refusing to be parted, her hands desperately helping as he undressed, a sharp gasp of pleasure leaving her lips as she felt at last the strong naked length of his body against her own, his arms strong and secure holding her against him.

'Oh, I have longed for you,' he whispered thickly. 'I have dreamed of you like this in my arms for such a long, empty time. I have wanted you and resisted you for as long as I can remember, since you were a shy and uncertain teenager. I have watched you grow and felt my pride and sanity slowly fading at the sight of you, afraid that something would happen to take you away from me, ashamed of my hunger for you.'

His lips trailed fire over her skin as she lay unresisting and warm in his arms, her own hands discovering places that brought shivers of pleasure to his body.

'You witch,' he whispered. 'You are smiling at me like a siren in the moonlight, beckoning me with your eyes and your lips, with your soft eager arms. You may bless the fact that you were shy and afraid for so long or I would have owned you years ago.'

'I wanted you to own me,' she whispered against his shoulder, her teeth biting into his strong muscles with tiny nipping bites.

'You were afraid,' he murmured, 'and I was too well schooled in protecting you to do anything but draw back. Nothing will protect you tonight, my beautiful nymph.'

With a hungry movement he found the hardened peaks of her breasts, darkened in the moonlight, lifting her to his searching lips and claiming them sensuously until she cried out in pain and pleasure, her body surging against his to be caught and held in bondage as he ravaged her with kisses, his strong hands finding all the secret places of pleasure, urging her on and slowing her down until she sobbed out her frustration against his demanding lips.

'I have waited for this, dreamed of this,' he muttered against her skin. 'Would you have it all ended swiftly? Would you have us fly into heaven and then return to earth?'

She locked her fingers behind his head, straining to find his mouth, her body arched and pleading, strange, despairing little cries on her lips that seemed to be coming from her with no thought behind them, only a need that hurt and ached, a fire that needed quenching now.

'You are glowing with beauty, alive with desire,' he breathed, his voice harsh and unsteady as he looked down at her with burning eyes. Her own eyes closed before the heat in his and she whispered his name in a sobbing plea.

'Ramón! Ramón!' Her body twisted frantically and he moved, his weight pressing her into the softness of the bed, his hands lifting her to him at last.

'Now, my sweet darling,' he breathed, tenderness in the harsh voice. 'Now I will make you whole and alive. Now you are mine.'

She cried aloud at the driving energy that possessed her, shuddering in ecstasy as the brief pain passed and warmth flooded her as he moved within her, his lips breathing her name as they fused with hers, his body moving with a new rhythm as they swiftly ascended to the heaven he had promised, until she tore her lips free to cry out his name in gladness.

They lay locked together when it was over, their legs entwined, their arms tightly around each other until their heart-beats steadied and he moved gently aside.

'Ramón!' Her sharp cry of fright had him laughing quietly as he pulled her into his arms and settled her against him, her head on his shoulder.

'I am not about to spring up and leave you,' he murmured, his lips moving softly against her heated face. He tilted her chin, forcing her to face him when she would have remained hidden against his strength. 'Regrets?' he asked softly, his dark eyes searching her face as they had done so often to read her moods.

'No.' Meriel shook her head, looked away and then swiftly back at him. 'Do you have regrets, Ramón?' she asked with anxious eyes on his face.

'You mean do I feel worried that I allowed myself for once in my life to follow my desires and take what I wanted?' He cupped her face with one warm, bronzed hand. 'You could have sent me away, but you did not. I would have waited for you, but I am happy that I did not have to because I know you so well. Now that you are really mine you will never go away from me.'

He pulled her back to him, pushing her head to his shoulder, enfolding her with warmth, tiredness claiming them both as they lay close together, drifting from one dream to another and finally sleeping. It was later in the night that the generator finally decided to come to life and Meriel stirred as the lamp she had vainly tried to switch on during the storm came on at last and shone in her face. She was cold too, wondering tiredly as she partially opened her eyes why she was sleeping on top of the clothes.

She turned her head on the pillow to find Ramón watching her with dark, burning eyes, his expression amused as colour flooded her face.

'You are cold?' he asked softly, moving the bedclothes to cover them both as she nodded. 'I would have covered you soon,' he said, 'but I wanted to look at you. Last night there was only the moon but I have now discovered that you are as beautiful in lamplight as you are in the moonlight. Come here,' he added huskily. 'Let me warm you, your skin is chilled worse than mine but together we will generate warmth.'

'Should—should you go back to your room?' she asked, hiding her eyes under the thickness of her lashes.'

'Should I?' he countered, his hand stroking down the length of her body, signalling his growing need to her as he moulded her against him.

'No,' she moaned as he nibbled her skin, his legs twining with hers, his lips searching urgently for her mouth. 'Suppose that Manolito comes in in the morning?' she whispered shakily as he turned her until she was looking up into the glitter of his eyes as he hovered over her.

'He will not.' Ramón's voice was almost dreamlike, his mind on nothing but his desire to possess her again. 'If he should do so, then I will explain to him about the birds and the bees and . . .' His voice trailed away as he looked down at her and her breathing choked in her throat at the naked desire on his face. 'I think that when I look at you, I will always desire you,' he said, his voice harsh and thrilling. 'It is a hunger that a hundred years will not assuage.'

She moved where he led, her head flung back to allow his mouth to search the slender arch of her neck, her body willing and eager to belong to him again, her mind too lost in the wonder of it to question why his words were passion and not love. She would have to live without love, but he was beautiful to her, perfect in every way, and her love was strong enough for both of them.

CHAPTER EIGHT

MANUEL did not come into her room the following morning but in any case it would not have mattered, Ramón was gone. Meriel lay in bed for a long time after she had awakened, her mind attuning itself to the reality of what had happened. Ramón had used no persuasion with her; on the contrary, in the stark light of day, it seemed to Meriel's anxious mind that she had initiated it all, moving from her terror of the storm to a different kind of storm that had grown in her heart and mind when Ramón held her and comforted her. No man, she supposed, would have been able to resist such temptation.

Guilt and embarrassment began to eat away at her until she forced herself out of bed, away from the tell-tale imprint of Ramón's head on her pillow and into the bathroom to shower. It would have been easier to face him here in this room than to go into the rest of the house and meet his dark eyes. She still could not throw off the feeling that she had held all her life that Ramón was her protector and superior, her stepbrother, the one who controlled her days. Her years in England had not rid her of the awe she felt about him, the feeling that he was some unattainable god. Now they were lovers. Her face flushed at the thought, and though it also brought a weakening warmth to her limbs it did nothing to ease away the enormity of it all.

He was not there. Her relief to find the breakfast-room empty and to know that she was to be served alone was so great that her legs shook and she sank into her chair with a sigh of gratitude.

'Señor Ortiga ordered that you were to be left to sleep,' Rosita announced with an air of mischief that made Meriel's cheeks flare with colour. 'He said that the storm had frightened you badly and that you were awake for most of the night.'

'Yes, I'm still afraid of the *tormenta*,' Meriel managed to get out in some resemblance to an easy manner. 'Señor Ortiga came home last night. He told me that the cattle would have to be moved today.'

'*Sí*, the men are out now and Señor Ortiga is with them but he will be back soon, I think. He is going to Caracas.'

'Yes.' Meriel looked away and began to eat. The confidences had gone far enough as far as she was concerned, and Rosita's eyes were bright with interest. The Caracas trip was for her dress, her wedding-gown. She didn't want to talk about it at all. Maybe now Ramón would not be so eager to go, maybe he would despise her for her desire to belong to him. It was so impossible to believe with the sun shining through the open windows and the room empty except for herself.

She heard Rosita's heels clicking on the tiles of the passage again and steeled herself to withstand more bright-eyed interrogation, but she was not to be subjected to any.

'There is a visitor for you, Señorita Meriel!' It was clear that this last incident had made Rosita's day. 'It is Señor Mackensie, the very one that I myself spoke to on the telephone. He has come from England to see you!'

'Stewart?' Meriel jumped up in astonishment, her actions satisfying Rosita, who clearly thought that this unexpected visitor deserved such a flurry of activity. She stood by hopefully but Meriel rushed out to the hall and stopped in a disturbing mixture of happiness, worry and surprise to see Stewart Mackensie standing tall and threatening in the open doorway.

'Meriel!' He strode forward but she could see at a glance that he was only just in control of his considerable temper and she hastily motioned him to the *sala* with one warning glance at him that indicated Rosita who stood with wide dark eyes watching, very willing to be enlightened.

'What the devil is going on here?' Stewart grasped her

arms as soon as the door was shut and towered over her suspiciously. 'Are you a prisoner here or something, Meriel? What's all this rubbish about resigning?'

'I've been trying to get in touch with you, Stewart, but nobody seemed to know where you were ...'

'I took off as soon as Ortiga phoned me,' he grated. 'I rang straight back and got him again. You were ill in bed, he said! My God, I thought he'd killed you and hidden the body! I drove straight to the airport and more or less camped out until I could get a plane here. The rest of the time I've been trying to find the damned place!'

'Stewart ...'

'What the hell are you doing still here in the back of beyond, Meriel? And what's all this resigning nonsense?'

He looked about as easy to handle as a mad bull, and she found herself eyeing him warily. She had seen his temper in action before but never at such close quarters and never as it was now, half directed at herself.

'I have resigned, Stewart,' she began as steadily as possible. 'I've written to confirm it and I've written a letter to you personally too but the post here ...'

'What the hell are you talking about, Meriel? Resigning! You're at the peak of your career! The Paris contract is the biggest thing we've picked up yet! You're going to be a director of the Mackensie Press yourself before too long! Do you realise your success? At your age it's little short of miraculous. The whole bloody place is falling apart! I will not accept your resignation!'

'You have little choice, Señor Mackensie!' The cool voice from the doorway made shivers run down Meriel's spine. Her back was to the door and Stewart was too enraged to notice even if an elephant had sauntered into the room. 'She is home and here she stays! The Mackensie Press will have to cope without their miracle-worker, she can be a director of the Ortiga Estates if she craves that kind of satisfaction.'

He was keeping his voice even, almost casual, but Meriel could hear the anger burning deep inside and a further shiver raced down her spine as he approached. She didn't turn her head but she knew exactly when he was close, had readily anticipated the arms that came round her from behind to draw her close to the hard and seething anger of his body. She glanced fearfully at the brown arms that lashed around her waist, the brown hands that captured her own, her eyes lifting them to the astonished anger on Stewart's face.

'Tell him, my darling,' Ramón suggested softly. 'If you can now slide in a word edgeways, tell him why you are not returning to England and the Mackensie Press.'

'I—I'm getting married,' Meriel burst out breathlessly. God, even with Stewart here glaring at them like a Viking marauder her legs were turning to water because Ramón was holding her against him. 'Ramón and I—we—we're getting married next week.'

Stewart Mackensie's mouth opened to speak but for a second even he was speechless. Not for long, though, his brow darkened like thunder and his blue eyes flashed with rage and suspicion at Ramón.

'What have you been doing to her? What sort of brow-beating has been going on here? Don't expect me to believe this monstrous arrangement. She hates you!'

'Do you, *pequeña*?' Ramón lifted his hand to tilt her face to his. 'Do you hate me?' His eyes were mocking and piercing and to her great shame he began to search her face with looks that caressed her wherever they fell, lingering on her tremulous mouth like a lover's kiss.

'She's your stepsister!' Stewart blurted out, shocked and enraged by this subtle but obvious lovemaking.

'Part of my past and all of my future!' Ramón's eyes, no longer teasing and amused, turned like fire on the man who raged in front of them. 'You have the resignation, Señor Mackensie! When you return to England no doubt there will be a letter waiting for you confirming it. If Meriel's unexpected resignation has broken her contract, then I will recompense you in whatever way is necessary, but be in no doubt that she will be my wife within a very short time and she will not return to England!'

'I don't know what he's said to persuade you, Meriel,' Stewart said, his voice now calm and the anger draining away by the second, 'but you know how I feel. There's nothing to be afraid of. You can walk out now if you wish and come with me.'

'You are a day too late, Señor Mackensie,' Ramón assured him with silken menace. 'She is already mine, perhaps even now bearing the heir to the Ortiga Estates.'

'You bastard!' Stewart's rage flared again as he glared with clenched fists at Ramón's darkly furious face. 'For your information, I don't care. I don't give a damn what happened yesterday. If Meriel wants to come with me then that is a part of her life that can be wiped out permanently!'

'She is not going with you, or anyone else!' Ramón rasped, his dark eyes flaring into rage, his arms tightening on Meriel to the point of pain.

'I'd like to know how you propose to stop her if she wants to go. What would you do? Kill her?' Stewart's contemptuous voice seemed only to calm Ramón's anger and his voice was merely matter-of-face when he replied.

'No. I would kill you. You would never leave the *llanos*, and do not doubt that for one minute. I have waited for her and at last she is mine. You have, I think, been a good friend to her, be content with that, it is all you can ever be and I will not attempt to sever that friendship, but Meriel is mine.'

'Meriel?' Stewart looked at her steadily, a new expression on his face that she could not really read but she forced her eyes to meet his.

'I want to marry Ramón, of my own free will. I'm sorry, Stewart, I never meant to hurt you, I never expected you to come here and I never ...'

'I know.' He suddenly sighed and his fine shoulders relaxed. 'I've always been a bull at a gate. I'll go.'

'You are welcome to stay,' Ramón cut in, releasing

Meriel and leaving her to stand as best she could on trembling legs. 'I have raged at people before and found them quite civilised later.'

'So have I,' Stewart laughed ruefully. 'Maybe we've got something in common after all, but I really need to go. The office will be in turmoil if I'm not there soon.'

He held out his hand and Ramón clasped it with a smile. 'I can't say the best man has won,' Stewart said ruefully. 'I wanted to win myself and I've got a hell of an opinion of my own importance. Just be good to her.' He hugged Meriel and turned to the door and she made to follow, Ramón making no attempt to stop her. Stewart did that, taking her firmly by the shoulders and planting her securely where she had been.

'Stay here, my dear,' he begged softly. 'I'm not into torture. If ever you need anything, I'm the man.' He strode out and she found tears flooding her eyes and turning away she ran out of the room into her bedroom to sit weeping quietly on the edge of the bed.

She heard Ramón come in but he said nothing and it was not for a few seconds that she felt the comforting warmth of his arms. She pulled away, suddenly angry with him for the scene that she had endured, knowing that he had not caused it but blaming him nevertheless.

'Why did you say that to Stewart?' she demanded wildly, her eyes silver and accusing in her pale face. 'Why did you tell him about about . . .'

'About the fact that we have been lovers?' he asked calmly. 'When I fight, I fight with every weapon at my disposal. I suppose to your English mind I am—what is the word? A cad. He took it however in a way that surprised me. He is truly worth having as a friend.'

'He's good and kind, even if he does rage sometimes,' she sniffed, wiping her eyes and then looking at him with moody anger. 'What would you have done if the positions had been reversed? What would you have done if he had blurted out the same thing?'

'Ah! You wish to know if I am good and kind?' He grasped her chin with strong fingers, his eyes flaring with anger even at the thought. 'I would have killed him and brought you—home!' He stared at her white face for a second and then stood abruptly. 'Get ready. We are flying to Caracas to get your wedding-gown. The sooner you are in it and married to me the sooner I shall be able to get on with my affairs. I wish to have that ring on your finger before any other would-be suitor makes an unexpected appearance. Manuel is off on an expedition with his teacher as you know so we will not be troubled by him.'

'I might be a long time looking for it,' she murmured, not standing up, stubbornness filling her that did not amuse him.

'You will have all the most expensive shops at your disposal!' he snapped. 'It will not be necessary to shop around. You can do your shopping in the day. I already have the ring.'

'In England,' she began heatedly,' the bride likes very often to help to choose the ring and . . .'

His opinion was blunt and brought a blush to her cheeks as he turned to the door.

'What about the cattle, about moving them?' she stammered, surprised that he was leaving everything to take her to Caracas. Apparently his opinion was very similar in that direction too and he walked out, slamming the door. She still sat there, angry and confused, jumping guiltily as he strode back in a second later, hauling her to her feet and looking down at her moodily.

'Get ready,' he muttered, his eyes flashing over her possessively, and when she simply stared up at him he suddenly pulled her into his arms, caressing her roughly and kissing her with a kind of savage delight that made her gasp.

'I just remembered that in the turmoil of Señor Mackensie's arrival I have not kissed you good morning,' he murmured against her lips. 'You have no more than twenty minutes, after that I will get you ready myself.'

She found the gown that she wanted almost at once, a delicious creation of cream satin and lace, the skirt looped and frilled like a ball-gown of days long past, and for a few minutes as she tried it on her mind eased of its worries. Soon, she would stand beside Ramón in a flower-bedecked *hacienda*, her father looking on as she vowed the rest of her life to him. Her happiness faded though as soon as she had dressed in her normal clothes. Ramón had been silent on the flight, in fact he had spoken not one word except to fill her bag with money and tell her to spend it all. She did, buying dresses that would be beautiful for a honeymoon even though she imagined that there would be no honeymoon. Ramón had made no mention of one.

He hardly spoke either on the way back and it was dark when they arrived at the *hacienda*, as dark as the eyes that watched her as she said good night in a small, uneven voice and fled to her room to toss and turn for a whole sleepless night, remembering the night before, reliving the thrill of his arms and worrying about his silence and dark, brooding looks.

He was there when she went to breakfast the next morning much earlier than her usual time, unable to linger in bed any longer, and his eyes were as tired as hers.

'You did not sleep.' He stated it with certainty as she came into the room and when she did not answer he grasped her hand as she passed his chair, holding her wrist tightly and looking up at her drawn face. 'Neither did I.'

He pushed his chair back and stood over her, his hands on her shoulders as he looked down into her face.

'Why did you not sleep?' he asked quietly, turning her face to the light when she did not answer. 'All right. I will tell you why I did not sleep. I wanted you in my bed and it is not a new feeling. Now that I have held you and possessed you, though, it is a more difficult feeling to conquer and I did not do very well in my battle with the lonely night.'

She turned wide grey eyes on him and he smiled at her quick flush of shyness.

'You wanted me to come for you?' he asked softly, laughing quietly at her quick action to hide behind lowered lashes. 'It is idiotic, is it not?' he said, 'two people in the same house, both with the same hunger and the strings of the past holding them apart. Had you not been who you are, I would have come in the night and taken you to the warmth of my bed.' He shrugged ruefully at her quick glance of surprise, his hands sliding into her hair and raising her face to his. 'The other night,' he said softly, 'was not the same. It was unpremeditated and unavoidable, like an instant fire, but now I must wait for you. This wedding had better be very soon, though,' he sighed, pulling her into his arms and resting his head against her hair.

He would never know how happy those few words made her feel and she waited now with a glowing face for the day of her wedding. Ramón was still obsessed with his need to protect her, even from himself, and she had no doubt that this would go when he realised that she was his wife, his to hold and keep for ever.

Her father arrived the day before to stay in one of the many luxurious rooms that the *hacienda* possessed, and her heart-beats steadied back to normal when it became clear that Ramón had accepted him, a little stiffly perhaps but none the less with kindness and courtesy, more kindness than she felt towards the other guests who began to arrive, relatives she had dreaded seeing for more years than she cared to remember. Not the least of these, by any means, were Doña Barbara and Carmen, both stiffly polite, kissing her cheeks like ice maidens and thereafter ignoring her. Consuelo Sandoval too was a guest, arriving with her father, a tall, dark man with cold eyes and an autocratic bearing that spoke of wealth and power and a steely determination to have his own way.

Her father noted them with his usual amusement and commented when they were all in the *sala* after dinner that night, so many guests around them that finding a corner to talk quietly was difficult.

'From earlier descriptions,' he murmured in her ear, 'I take it that the stiffly upright dragon of an old lady is the dreaded Aunt Barbara, her escort Carmen?'

'True,' she sighed, her eyes on them as they collared a none-too-pleased Ramón. 'They're now about to try and tell Ramón how he should do things.'

'Poor foolish souls!' her father laughed. 'He's like a rock-face, he even looks capable of crushing them too. I bet he only has to use a few words to get them off his back.'

He actually laughed outright when the expected happened and Tia Barbara stalked away with an outraged Carmen beside her. Ramón chose that moment to look across at them, his frown not lifting as he saw Meriel, her father's arm around her, both of them laughing happily. It took a great deal of effort to keep the smile on her face as he began to make his way towards them purposefully and towered over them, his face moody and tight.

'Come and walk with me on the terrace,' he said in little less than an outright order. 'I'm sure that your father will survive for a few minutes, in fact I can see Manuel making his way determinedly over here and no doubt he is anxious to recapture your father.'

It was true, Manolito had taken a great liking to her father and stayed resolutely beside him whenever he had the chance. So she nodded and went out to the terrace, having little alternative anyway with his hand clasping her possessively.

'He is younger than I expected,' Ramon said as they stepped off the veranda and walked into the gardens. 'He is fair too; I am beginning to gain the impression that all the men in your life are fair!'

'They come in all shapes, sizes and colours,' Meriel quipped, more to escape from the tight feeling that restricted her throat than to make amusing comments. He swung her round and into his arms with frightening speed, his hands cupping her startled face immediately.

'They'd better not come at all!' he bit out, watching her for an angry second before suddenly laughing softly. 'You can get under my skin with one little comment, do you know that? I am dying of frustration, irritated by the crowds of people who are separating me from you and on guard constantly in case your father decides suddenly to take you and make a run for it.'

'He approves of the match,' she said, her breath uneven as she looked up at him. 'He knows I want to marry you and he wants me to be happy. He's not a selfish man.'

'And I am?' he asked quietly, his hands beginning to trace her face, his body moving closer in the warm night air.

'I never said that and I didn't think it,' she muttered, looking away from the gleam of his eyes. 'I was making a point about my father.'

He said nothing, simply continuing to caress her face with a trembling kind of touch that spoke of his hunger for her, his body hardening and adjusting to hers when she swayed forward and leaned against him.

'Ramón?' She looked up into his dark eyes, almost afraid by what she saw there and his lips brushed hers, moving back and forth in a teasing and exciting demand.

'Sleep with me tonight,' he murmured against her mouth. 'You're an obsession! I can't take my eyes from you. I can't sleep or eat. I've got years of desire to satisfy, years of watching you and imagining how you would be in my arms.'

'You didn't!' she gasped against his open mouth as he waited to devour her.

'I did! I wanted you until I almost hated you. Certainly I hated myself. Only the knowledge that one day I would take you kept me sane, that and the duty I owed you, but it was a very thin line that we walked, my little witch.'

The waiting lips swooped to claim hers, this time savagely, demandingly, his mouth smothering her cry as he tightened her to him in a crushing embrace that was all desire and no affection at all. She was a woman he craved and the depths of his craving were all too apparent.

'Now!' he muttered harshly, swinging her up into his arms as if she were merely feather-light. 'We will go in through the back door, there are so many guests here that no one will even notice our absence.'

'No! Ramón!' She plucked frantically at his shoulders and he stopped, looking down at her, his eyes glazed with desire.

'You want me!' he said harshly! 'I can feel it running inside you like the river at flood-time.'

'I do—do want you, but not like this,' she whispered, pleading with him. It was not necessary however to plead, and what his response would have been she did not know because another voice called to him from the shadows, the soft, throaty voice of Consuelo Sandoval, and he stiffened with annoyance and frustration, setting Meriel down on trembling legs that threatened to allow her to fall, his arm still painfully tight around her.

'Ramón, my father wishes to have a quiet word with you.' She faltered when she saw who was with him, noticing Meriel's wildly flushed face and the tight restraint on Ramón's. 'I—I'm sorry. I—I didn't know that . . . I thought you were alone.'

'Alone!' His bark of laughter was bitter and rather cruel. 'That is an impossibility, I think, tonight. However, I will speak to your father, though how our words can be quiet words is beyond me!'

He left them both, striding off into the house without a backward glance and Consuelo moved towards Meriel, her face embarrassed.

'I'm sorry, Meriel,' she said softly, clearly meaning it. 'I should have known better than to come out but my father can be very angry when he chooses.'

'Don't worry.' Meriel had regained some measure of composure. 'I know all about very angry, Ramón is not short of a temper himself.'

'I know.' Consuela looked after Ramón with dark, veiled eyes. 'I have known him for a long time, as you will remember. Passion like his can be wildly consuming.'

She said nothing else and they returned to the house together but a little part of Meriel had suddenly frozen to ice. Did Consuelo know Ramón so well that she too had felt his passion? If that were to be taken away from her there would be nothing left but the past. She was more frightened than she had ever been before.

The wedding was early and Meriel did not come out of her room that morning at all until the time for the ceremony. Rosita herself had served her breakfast in bed although she had been too tight inside to eat much of it. She had seen nothing of Ramón before bedtime last night and he had simply gone to his room and left her in hers. He had been in the study with Señor Sandoval for the rest of the evening and she had been glad of the soothing company of her father and Manolito who hung around until late, consuming every word that her father uttered until the whole thing became laughable.

She took one final look at herself in the mirror, her face faintly flushed with anxiety, her grey eyes large and clear but a faint fear in their depths. The beautiful dress was like a dream against her skin and the opal like a talisman hanging between her breasts. She had not allowed herself to think deeply about the words that had come without thought from Consuelo the night before but the tightening around her heart was a pain that would not go away.

Overnight, the house had been transformed. There were banks of flowers everywhere and she knew that the servants must have been up for most of the night to arrange the rooms for her wedding day. They were there too, lining the long passage way that led to the *sala* as Meriel walked beside her father, her hand on his arm, her fingers clenching and unclenching anxiously until he covered them with his own to calm her.

The doors at the end of the *sala* had been thrown open to add to the spaciousness and make the adjoining room available too but all she really saw, all she really remembered later, was Ramón, his face peculiarly still, his eyes too dark and deep to read as he watched her come towards him on this morning that would commit her to his life forever.

It passed in a dream, Meriel's world contracting to one man and the vows they both made, and only as they turned did the faces of the assembled guests take on any meaning. There was a strange kind of satisfaction on the face of Doña Barbara that puzzled her, but the face of Consuelo Sandoval was no puzzle at all. There were tears in her eyes that threatened to roll down her cheeks and shame her before everyone. Meriel wondered what self-destructive motive could have made her come to see Ramón married to another when she was so clearly in love with him herself. She glanced beneath her lashes at Ramón but he was not looking at Consuelo, he was looking at her, a smiling triumph in his eyes that lifted her heart.

There was a surprise in store for her too. When the meal was over and the toasts made, Ramón announced that he and his bride would be leaving within the hour.

'Leaving?' Meriel looked up at him as he stood tall and handsome at her side.

'*Sí*, leaving!' He smiled down at her and took her hand. 'You did not imagine that we would be taking our honeymoon at the *hacienda*, I hope?'

'I didn't think that . . .'

'We are going to Mexico,' he said softly, his eyes flashing over her startled face. 'Many times you have expressed the wish to go there and this is a very good time to take you.'

'Oh, Ramón!' Her face lit up with pleasure, all her worries cast aside, and he took her hand to his lips, smiling at her happiness, a great tenderness in him.

'I will always try to please you,' he said softly. 'I only

want to be near you.' Manuel was bursting with the news, almost bouncing with joy at their side.

'It was a secret, Merry,' he informed her. 'Only Ramón and I knew, but later of course we had to tell your father, Ramón and I picked out the hotel, we arranged the flight and everything!' He was bubbling with pride and Ramón gazed down at him with severity that was covering laughter.

'It is my wedding day,' he said firmly. 'You will have to stand back for a while.'

'Carmen and I will stay to take care of Manuel!' Ramón's aunt announced in a voice that allowed for no argument, but Ramón turned to her with his charming smile that hid so much.

'Your kindness is so constant, Tía Barbara,' he said quietly, 'and of course I thought of asking you, but it is so isolated here and I decided that it was not reasonable to place you in such a situation. Meriel's father has agreed to stay, to take a week's holiday and keep an eye on Manuel. Señor Morales too has agreed to move into the house for a short time. He will be here every day to teach Manuel so it is more convenient that he stay here for the time being. With his presence and the presence of Señor Curtis, I think Manuel will be well supervised.'

There was an audible gasp from Ramón's aunt before she managed to control her shock and chagrin, and Meriel caught her father's eye, seeing that he was having a great deal of difficulty in containing his ready laughter. Even Señor Morales had an unexpected twinkle in the depths of his normally sombre gaze.

'When did you arrange all this?' she whispered to her father when she had a minute to get him alone.

'Soon after I came,' he said, dropping his voice to conspiratorial level. 'Manuel asked me outright and I think Ramón was somewhat embarrassed by the sheer cheek of it, but oddly enough, quite pleased when I agreed. Señor Morales seems to be rather tickled by the events, I take it that he knows the aunt?'

'Don't we all?' Meriel whispered. 'She'll not take this lying down.'

'With your husband in charge, I really think she has no choice at all.' The word husband rang oddly in Meriel's ears and she turned to look at Ramón to find his eyes intently on them both, a question deep in the gleam of them, his expression only lightening when she flushed and smiled shyly.

'I still cannot work out exactly what I am to you now, Meriel,' Manuel commented later when they were almost about to change for their trip.

'I would think that the word "burden" would probably do,' Ramón teased. 'For a whole week she is rid of you. I can see relief written all over her face.' Of course Manuel knew it was not true. He was happy as she had never seen him, and she knew that with her father there and the watchful and strict eyes of Arturo Morales upon him he would be quite safe. They left soon after to fly to Caracas and on to Mexico and Ramón did not seem disposed to release her hand for more than a few seconds throughout the journey. She was happy, safe, her wildest dreams a reality.

Even though it would not be the first time, her shyness overwhelmed her as the night drew near and they danced together in the ballroom of the hotel where they were staying. It was luxurious as everywhere that Ramón stayed was luxurious, and she was glad of the dresses she had bought.

He danced, as he did everything else, expertly, beautifully, and he was silent as only he could be. Her body followed his movements with an unthinking grace, his breath against her cheek, every movement he made adding to her desire to melt against him, her senses attuned to the aching that was raging inside him too.

'It's time to go to bed,' he said abruptly, making a chill shiver over her.

'I I want to—can't we dance a little longer?'

'Yes, if you want me to make love to you here in front of these nice, respectable people,' he murmured derisively. He drew back and looked at her flushed face and then pulled her back against him. 'It's not the same, is it? The first time was like being in an avalanche. I did warn you, if you remember.'

'You—you mean that now it's—it's cold-blooded?'

His mouth quirked as he lifted his head back and looked into her anxious face.

'Naturally,' he taunted. 'With nothing surprising left and the need to be gentle gone it leaves only my— obsession.'

'Ramón! I'm frightened—I . . .'

'Shut up,' he said softly. 'There's only one place that will cure your fright.'

He swung her round, his arm tightly holding her as he led her from the floor to the lift. Safely inside, he did not touch her. He stood against the wall, watching her with a mounting amusement that brought swift colour under her skin as the lift rose rapidly to the suite of rooms at the top of the hotel. Even inside the comfort of the sitting-room, the lamplight soft and soothing, he still said nothing, and she walked to the great window to look out over the lights of the city, her heart-beats threatening to choke her. Her father had called him her husband and he was that in reality, but his silence, his power spoke only of Ramón, a dark handsome man who had ruled her life for so long, an almost alien being who had been her protection, her teacher, her tormentor for all the years she had been away from England. This was no handsome stranger she had married, and there was so much past in their relationship that she was too frightened to respond in any way. He was not helping at all, his silence cruel and amused, laughing at her timidity as he had done for so many years.

She sensed him behind her and stiffened when his hands drew her back to him. There was no way now that she could lean against him and she could not imagine what mad yearning had led her to take the initiative after the storm.

He clearly expected nothing though, turning her in his arms and holding her close with a gentleness that was devoid of all passion, stroking her back in a soothing rhythm, finding the tense muscles beneath the heavy fall of her hair and massaging them with warm fingers.

Subtly, his silence was no longer one of amusement, it was sensuous, coaxing, his body closer and in harmony with hers, tightening against her as she began to move closer, taking its lead from her and accepting each movement she made.

He was ready when she slowly raised heavy-lidded eyes to his, a dazed look beginning to come over her pale face, but he made no move to claim her mouth. His hands traced the contours of her body, his lips brushed her face until she lowered her head as if it were heavy from sleep.

'Look at me,' he whispered thickly. 'Look at me and ask yourself what you see.' She saw Ramón, a man she had loved in one way or another for most of her life, a man whose taut face was holding in a raging desire, whose dark eyes ate into her soul, and her breath was a little sob in her throat.

'Do you know that your shyness is a lure to me?' he asked, his breath harsh in his throat. 'I am looking into the same eyes that I looked into so long ago when I wanted you like a mad fool. What do you fear, Meriel? Are you so lost in the past that you feel this is unreal, that I am merely someone who guards and protects you? I do not want that. We are equals or we are nothing and if we are nothing then my hunger for you is wrong, merely an animal instinct.'

There was pain on his face that even outshone the desire and her arms lifted to hold him tightly, her body moving into his with a desperate urgency of its own.

'Oh, Meriel!' He swept her up into his arms and carried her across the room, his lips hot on her shoulder as she wound herself around him, her whole being enslaved as he undressed her gently and moved with her into a timeless enchantment, their movements a slow and passionate ritual in the lamplit room, touching each other, looking into each other's eyes as if to be separated would be to die. There was no sound except their breathing, Ramón's face dark with passion, his hands gentle and thrilling, and Meriel too had no wish to speak, she only wanted to look at him, to touch him and to love him.

Even his final possession of her was silent, the feelings too deep for words, a tender violence that left her floating in the outer spaces of time even when he had returned to earth. She knew too that he had not shown the depths of his passion, he had taken her with a gentle protection that left him still filled with longing.

'Don't go!' She turned to him urgently when he stirred and saw his smile, half wistful in the lamplight.

'I am well disciplined, accustomed to hardship,' he said softly, 'but to leave you now would be the end of me. I am still hungry, you know that?'

He cupped her face in his hands, his eyes searching hers deeply.

'I know. I know more about you than you think. Even though you shutter your eyes against me.'

'Do I do that?' he asked, smiling faintly, his hands moving over her with an impatience that she recognised and thrilled to. 'Perhaps if I did not you would be more timid and shy. Perhaps you would see how I really want you.'

'I'm not timid,' she assured him, breathlessly, her eyes holding his. 'I know how you want me and I'm not made of silk.'

'It seems so to me,' he breathed, his hands moving in dark exploration over her. 'You are so pale, so fair, so very, very—different.' He stared into her eyes and she fought the desire to hide from him, knowing his need and looking back fearlessly until his breathing was a hard rasp in his throat, and he moved with deliberate pressure over her, then with a muttered word his mouth found hers and she was drawn tightly beneath him, his arms crushing her possessively as passion leapt from him and flooded her too. There was a craving inside him that had been bottled up for years and she heard his harsh intake of breath as she moved convulsively beneath him, wanting to prove that she was everything he needed. Their bodies burning with heat, they moved together until the feelings became too much to bear and she cried out in a helpless moan of sound that was a plea and a signal all together. Then he lifted her tightly to him, invading her with a hungry urgency that was like nothing she had ever imagined, a depth that reached her soul and beyond, that held her with him to soar into a rapture that was colour and light and timeless.

His breathing steadied at last and he lifted his head to smooth the damp hair from her face, a contentment on his face that she had never seen before.

'You will be bruised tomorrow,' he said with little sigh of regret.

'So will you,' she murmured, her long, thick lashes flickering down to cover her eyes. 'One of these days, I'll really show you who's boss.'

His laughter released the tension and he turned to his side pulling her with him and enfolding her closely, his hand beneath her chin as he raised her face to look at her closely.

'You are afraid now, my sweet Meriel?' he asked softly and she shook her head.

'No.' She stroked his face with gentle fingers. 'For the first time, I really know you. I've got a wonderful feeling of power.' She smiled up at him impishly. 'I'll soon be able to call you to heel.'

He rocked her against him, laughing softly, and she rested contentedly in his arms. 'Yes,' he sighed. 'You are—different, and you fulfil all the promise in your eyes. Make me another promise, Meriel. Be happy.'

It was an odd thing to say at a time like this but she knew with a little burst of anxiety that he often knew her more than she knew herself. He noticed every expression that crossed her face and he looked for her needs. She wanted nothing but his love, and the strained, beautiful face of Consuelo came unbidden into her mind as she nestled against him. Would there be a reason for unhappiness? She prayed not and her arms tightened around him, her lips almost ready to ask outright the question that had hovered there for so long, but his breathing was deep and soft, he was asleep.

She raised herself to look into his face, a face she had dreamed of for so long in her life, and there were no lines of harshness on it, no strain. He was satisfied, content, his strong arm around her waist as if it would never move from her for the rest of his life. She kissed his lips gently and he stirred, tightening his grip, his mouth smiling with a softness that was almost boyish.

'Meriel.' He breathed her name sleepily and then was lost to her in the dreams that came in the warm darkness of night.

CHAPTER NINE

FLYING over the *llanos* a week later, Meriel sat contentedly beside her husband. Things were different. They were both rested and tanned, more at ease with each other than they had ever been before. The week had been days of laughter, nights of love, a week over far too soon because she didn't want to share Ramón with anyone, not even with Manolito. Every minute had been a cherished time to stay in her memory for the rest of her life.

'Look, the last of the cattle being moved. They've managed well.'

Ramón pointed down through the window to where she could see a small herd being driven across the flat savanna towards the higher land that was the foothills of the mountains, the men trailing behind and then moving to the flanks to contain the straggling herd.

'How do you know that they're the last?'

'Because today is Friday and this is the day the last were supposed to be moved,' he said wryly. 'If there are more dotted about, somebody is going to have a few awkward questions to answer.'

He suddenly banked the plane and flew out over the grasslands to the south, skimming low, hopping over dry trees and unusual outcrops of rocks, touring the area and giving her a glimpse of the land she had never seen.

'You're expecting to find some cattle?' she asked in amusement, but he glanced at her and laughed.

'No! I'm giving you a view of your kingdom. You did say that one day you would show me who is boss. You had better see exactly what you are boss of.'

Remembering the content of her remarks and the time they were said, Meriel blushed wildly and he grinned, his

160

hand leaving the controls to stroke her face.

'What do you think?' he asked. 'Does your kingdom please you?'

'I had no idea quite how isolated we were,' she breathed, not a little in awe at the vast stretches of land that spread below them. 'I'm so used to thinking in terms of the *hacienda*, and then the plane to the city that the area around has never really had more than a dreamlike quality.'

'And now it is a nightmare?' he asked, only half in jest.

'If it is, then you're in it,' she smiled. 'I'll settle for that nightmare any day.' She leaned across and kissed his tanned cheek and he turned swiftly to kiss her lightly on the lips.

It was wonderful and as to the isolation, she would have been content in the high Andes, so long as Ramón was there.

'Well, at least you have the luxury of the house,' he said softly, seemingly picking his way among her thoughts.

'A wooden hut would do,' she laughed shyly, 'always provided that there was running water.'

'We will have as much running water as we can cope with before long, I think,' he answered ruefully, his eyes on the distant clouds. 'We have managed everything in good time but when your father has been taken back to Caracas, the higher airstrip will have to be used all the time.'

That silenced her for a while because she hadn't actually thought about her father for the whole week and now he would be going, and she had no idea when she would see him again. There was no pull now, though, between England and her new home. Ramón was here and that was all she would ever want. She smiled and said nothing as he shot her a dark-eyed glance of appraisal, his gaze questioning.

'If you want an answer to that comment, then—er—yes,' she said mischievously, and saw his quick smile as he brushed her chin with his fist.

He took her with him too the next day when her father

was flown to Caracas and caught the flight out of Venezuela, and she was touched by his consideration. He had left them alone for the better part of the evening before, allowing them to talk quietly together. At the airport too he had disappeared after a short while so that their goodbyes would be in private, and it was only as her father went through the last barrier and she turned away that she saw Ramón standing with unreadable eyes watching her.

'You did not cry!' he said in an almost accusing tone as she went to him.

'If you really want me to I could work myself up to it,' she quipped, a little shocked by his harsh voice, but relaxing immediately as his arm came tightly round her. There were still these dark and silent moments when she felt that she would never get to the stage when his whole mind was open to her, but it was easy to forget when his arms came around her.

The days were busy now, with much to do before the floods hit the flat plains and filled the river to the top of the deep banks, making it into a violent, raging being. There were also trips to make to the mines, and Ramón took up his duties as if he had never slackened the reins. Meriel hugged to herself the memories of their time in Mexico when she awoke to the feel of his lips on hers, spent the days with his arm possessively around her, for now she hardly saw him.

There were at first days of separation and then, suddenly, two weeks with no word from him. At first, when he had been spending just days away, he had telephoned, sometimes twice in the day, but now, he was silent, the phone never rang and the days were long and lonely.

There was Manuel, of course, and also Meriel had taken up her own duties as mistress of the *hacienda*. She had wished neither to make great changes nor to interfere but she was too accustomed to work simply to sit about, and after a couple of short tussles with Rosita, her place was established. It had taken a great deal of courage to assert herself in a house where she had always felt excluded from everything, but it had to be done.

She moved purposefully too into Ramón's study, re-organising things, sitting for hours reading through papers and filing things in a more orderly manner, gaining as she went a great insight into the vast wealth of the Ortigas and the great amount of work and responsibility that rested with Ramón.

She had started this project when he had first gone and had stood a little worried as he had surveyed the results with raised eyebrows but his quick laughter had wiped the anxiety from her face and he had looked down into her eyes as he held her and said with a great deal of satisfaction, 'I think that soon you will be ready for further duties. We will have to get you a place on the Board. I can then sometimes have a few days off and send you along in my place to argue.' She didn't know if he meant it but it was a great compliment, coming from Ramón.

During this long absence though it was hard to settle, her ears were straining all day and every day for the sound of a telephone that never rang, and finally she began to feel almost ill at the strain that Ramón's silence placed her under. Even food was hard to face and many times her breakfast was sent back untouched.

It was Rosita's concern that finally made her realise though that there was more than loneliness troubling her. She was one morning filled with a deep nausea that had her racing to her bathroom and leaning later exhausted by the sink. She opened her eyes to see the reflection of Rosita in the mirror, her face no longer worried but beaming with satisfaction.

'Ah! It is as I hoped, you are *encinta*! The *señor* will be filled with happiness!'

Pregnant! It was a thought that had not entered her head. She was used to irregularities and had thought that her flight to Mexico, the excitement, so many things would have been enough to explain her condition. She sat for almost an hour beside the bed, drinking the weak tea and dry toast that Rosita had forced on her, her heart fluttering with excitement, longing to tell Ramón and see his face. She did not get the chance, though, he remained out of contact, and though she knew that the news would spread like wildfire through the house, she told no one herself; there was no one she wanted to tell but Ramón.

It was towards the end of the second week when she came into the *sala* after one of her bouts of early-morning sickness to find Doña Barbara already seated there, her face oddly smug, her car waiting outside with her chauffeur. She did not intend to stay then, at least that was a relief, and Meriel summoned up every ounce of her courage and courtesy to face her.

'Why Tia Barbara, what a surprise! I'm afraid that Ramón is not here at the moment, though. I hope you didn't come all this way to see him.'

'No, Meriel. I came actually to see you and I am very glad that I did.'

There had been a brief burst of annoyance on her face as Meriel had addressed her as aunt but her overriding pleasure at something that Meriel could not even guess at soon chased away the quick frown.

'We could have coffee, if you like,' she began, urging herself on to be more sociable than she felt. In fact the unusual glee on the tight face opposite was beginning to fill her with a nameless dread. It was the first time ever that she had seen Doña Barbara looking pleased and she knew that this must mean trouble for somebody. Clearly that somebody was herself.

'No. We will dispense with the civilities and get down to the reason for my visit.' She settled herself in the chair, staring at Meriel with hard black eyes. 'You are pregnant!' she announced without further ado. 'Do not bother to deny it, I have the whole thing from Rosita who cannot hold her tongue on any occasion.'

'I was not about to deny it,' Meriel assured her quietly. 'I would have liked it though if Ramón could have been the first to know.'

'He has not telephoned you then?' There was actually a smile on the waspish face and Meriel felt her own face paling, her anger was rising too, and she was unsure how long she could keep up the façade of politeness with this woman who had always so clearly resented and disliked her. This now was her home and she was in charge of it.

'He does telephone, naturally but this week I imagine he has been too busy or is not close to a telephone. I would be very gratefully, Tia Barbara, if you would keep the information that Rosita has so obviously blurted out to you a strict secret until I can tell Ramón myself.'

'Are you sure, my dear, that this is a wise course?' The malice was uppermost now, drowning everything else. 'I really think it would be as well, from your point of view, to hang on to your little happiness as long as possible. When Ramón knows that the heir is assured then I think that your life will not be so very good here as it has perhaps become. You were always outside the family, naturally, and after the birth of any heir you will probably wish that you had stayed out of it altogether.'

'What do you mean?' Meriel's face was now as pale as snow, her stomach knotted with anxiety, waiting to hear the words that were so obviously the reason for this visit.

'You were always such a naïve child,' Doña Barbara sighed. 'If you had been in any way normal you would never have married Ramón, you would have seen what is so obvious to everyone else, that he loves another. You were always so stupid.'

'I think that you had better go.' Meriel stood, her hand still on the chair, needing all the support she could get as she faced the amused old eyes that were watching her with an indifferent and malicious gaze.

'Do not be so dramatic, child! I can see where Manuel has picked up his desire for drama, he has been with you far too often in England. It will be better when he sees you no longer and is back under Ramón's hand solely.'

She never moved from her chair but looked up with complete confidence in herself but it was this last remark that struck the final blow at Meriel's heart and her anger rose to the top.

'I am mistress now,' she said with a quiet anger, 'and I have asked you to leave!'

'I will leave. It was to be only a short visit and I have almost finished. You should in all fairness know what is going on, however. We are a cold and undemonstrative family but we are normally fair to all. It is unfortunate that such an uncared-for person as yourself should have been chosen as the sacrifice but again I can see Ramón's reasons and there has never been any doubt in my mind of his physical desire for you. This, however, is not love and, as I say, he has loved another for some considerable time, from the moment he saw her in fact.'

Meriel was unable to speak. Inside, she knew that this old woman was filled with wickedness, that this was her revenge on both herself and Ramón, but the face of Consuelo Sandoval came again into her mind, the words she had used, her tears at the wedding, Ramón's tight face and his convulsive clasp on her own hand.

'I can see by your eyes that you already know some of the truth, you always had the most expressive eyes, my dear,' Doña Barbara murmured triumphantly. 'Beautiful eyes really,' she put her head on one side and watched Meriel's face. 'It is a great pity, but Consuelo cannot ever have children and it is necessary, as you have always known. There is the inheritance. Now that an heir is assured I would imagine that Ramón will want to spend more time with Consuelo, perhaps finally to marry her. He was at great pains to arrange the marriage at the *hacienda* and not in the church, although the cathedral has always been the place of marriages for this family. Still he would not have wanted . . .'

'Get out!' Meriel stood wild-eyed, her finger pointing at the door. 'Get out! I am Ramón's wife! I am no longer an outsider, to be put aside at the whim of an Ortiga. While I live here you are never welcome! Get back on your broomstick, you wicked and bitter old woman!'

The hard face suffused with colour and Doña Barbara strode to the door, her final shot typical.

'While you live here,' she remarked harshly. 'I wonder how long that will be.'

Meriel stood like stone as she heard the car pull away, her mind numb. It was one thing to listen to her own logic and realise that this was not the way that Ramón would ever act. He had always protected her, always shielded her from hurt. He would never hurt her like this, a hurt that would be final. And yet, her heart told her, he had never said at any time that he loved her. He had wanted her for many years, that much he had admitted. And there was the inheritance, the Ortiga future, the passion that ran deep in this family, their constant link with the past.

She brushed aside Rosita and went to her room, her legs hardly able to carry her. Manuel was out for the day, another visit with Arturo Morales, his notebooks under his arm as he had driven off in Señor Morales' car. He would not be in until nightfall and there was nothing of comfort that she could have got from her brother in any case, she would never tell him this.

She thought of telephoning her father, of making a great attempt to find out where Ramón was, and finally she rang one of the mines.

'Señor Ortiga is at the other house, *señorita*. I can get a message to him. Who shall I say is calling?' The quiet voice came from far off but Meriel was silent, unwilling to disclose her identity to anyone, ashamed that she seemed to be unexpectedly checking up on Ramón. It had not been her intention.

'The other house?' She had heard of it though she had never seen it. It was smaller, less grand than this but one of the Ortiga homes that was rarely used. 'Can you give me the number?'

'I regret, *señorita*, that I cannot. Señor Ortiga left strict instructions that no one was to be given the number of the telephone at this house. It has been only recently connected and he wishes it to remain unknown. Perhaps Señorita Sandoval has this authority. I can give you her number although I fear she will not be at her own home. I myself saw her go to the house with Señor Ortiga early this morning.'

'Thank you.' How stupid, her mind said, how bizarre to thank someone who has just shattered your life. She sat by the telephone for a second and then went back to her room, their room, the room she shared so happily with Ramón, the room where he held her close in the darkness and overwhelmed her with his passion. She was too spent for tears.

It was much later that she got up and began to pack her cases, taking only two, all she felt was necessary, and all the plane would be likely to hold with her other bits and pieces. The clothes she had bought here were left, she never wanted to see them again.

Luck was with her too. From the window she saw Luis Silva and went out to him.

'I'm flying to Caracas in about two hours, Luis. Please get the car ready and then fly me there.' She used all her new authority, her face perfectly cool.

'*Sí*, Señora Ortiga.' His dark eyes scanned her face swiftly and he looked away again with the same speed. 'I have first an errand that must be done, it may be that it will be a little more than two hours before I can get back but I will then be here with the car and we will be off at once. I hope that this is satisfactory.'

'Very well, Luis, but hurry.'

He nodded and went on his way and she waited in a fever of anxiety. She knew that Ramón would have left him with jobs to do. Nobody here sat around idle. Also he would not have dared to disobey Ramón and take her off the *rancho* leaving his tasks uncompleted. She would have to wait, she only hoped that she would be away before Manolito came back. She could not tell him of Ramón's betrayal, he was only a child, and she could not stay and face Ramón, not now that she knew.

She was still pacing the floor when she heard the car and she was completely ready, her cream silk trouser suit a good outfit to travel to Caracas and then to England, her deep blue blouse unwittingly showing up the pallor of her face. There was only the jacket to put on and she could get Luis to fetch her things. She turned from the bed where it had been waiting and faced the door, a gasp of alarm and shock leaving her at the sight of Ramón, dark and furious, his frame filling the doorway, barring her passage.

Her hand went to her stomach in an unconsciously protective gesture that she had picked up as a little habit since she had realised that she carried Ramón's child inside her. As yet there seemed to be nothing to protect but the habit had grown and she was now afraid at the rage in those burning dark eyes.

'So!' he hissed angrily, his eyes going from her to her luggage and back again.' You have had your fill of the *llanos*! You are once again hearing the call of England, your father and the full life you lived there!'

He locked the door, his eyes never leaving hers as he turned the key, and fear threatened to choke her at such fury that raged across his normally impassive face.

'Luis betrayed me!' Stupidly it was all she could gasp out and it served only to heighten his fury.

'*Si*, he is as afraid to die as the next man. He has flown to the mine to bring me home. He knows better than to assist you in any flight. It would have been his last flight, he would have had wings of his own and well he knows it!'

'I won't stay here!' Her cry might be filled with panic but she was adamant. She could not stay here to be destroyed. Even now with fury on his face, her heart turned over at the sight of him, a sickness deep inside her that he felt nothing but passion, no spark of the love that she felt, not even it seemed a lingering affection now that she had defied him.

'The English rose is withering on the wild plains of Venezuela?' he queried bitterly. 'You have realised then your mistake in committing yourself to me and to this land? The idea of the floods, the storms, the isolation does not really appeal to you now that you have been left alone to think deeply? It comes to my mind that after our honeymooon you wished to live in a hut in order to be with me. How short-lived has been your commitment.'

She could not answer, could not bring herself to say the things that needed to be said. She loved him too much to see the proud face reduced to embarrassment by her accusations, and dreaded the alternative that he would tell her coldly that it was true and that she would have to live with the reality of it forever.

'You imagine that I will let you go?' he asked with a menacing quiet. 'Once you could have escaped me but not now, not ever. I have held you in my arms, owned you, felt your body beneath mine and I will feel it again even though you hate me.'

She backed away from him as he advanced, fear written across her face, her hand again going in the protective gesture to her still flat stomach. He stopped dead as if an invisible barrier had been thrown up between them, his own face suddenly pale and stricken.

'You are pregnant!' It wasn't a question. His eyes skimmed over her, resting on her hand that stayed flat and trembling against her body. 'You are carrying my child and you were prepared to flee from me and take the child with you!'

He pounced on her and grasped her shoulders, dragging her to him and staring into her wide and frightened eyes. She could see so many things in those eyes, rage, astonishment and oddly enough a pain that almost matched her own.

'You were prepared to fight me for possession of a child we made together?' he whispered harshly. 'You wish to see history repeat itself, another lonely and unhappy child torn between two ways of life, two worlds?'

'No!' She tore herself away, turning her back to him, tears beginning to well up into her eyes. She had given no thought to that aspect of the affair. She could not stand up as her mother had done and face Ramón as Inez had faced her father, coldly and logically fighting for a bewildered child, and he would fight, she had no doubt, but she could not let this part of him that she had go. It was all she would ever have.

'I—I won't ever do that,' she whispered brokenly. 'You're not like my father and I'm not like Inez. Somehow, we'll work it all out later. I won't deprive you of the baby.'

'You will not get the chance,' he murmured bitterly. 'I will not let you go. It is you that I want and though I never touch you again I will have you where I can see you for the rest of my life. When I made you mine it was permanent, forever, even before our marriage vows. I have not changed my mind!'

'I shall go, Ramón,' she said dully. 'You can't hold me here against my will and I think you know that perfectly well.'

She walked away from him to the high French windows, looking out at the sky, the distant mountains and the heavy thunder clouds that gathered like the black weight in her heart. 'Oh! If only it could have been different! If only it could have been real! I've trusted you all my life, believed every word you uttered, relied on your honesty and now ...'

'In what am I dishonest?' he said with tightly controlled anger, his voice just behind her although she had never heard him move.

'I—I have no desire to embarrass you, Ramón, and you can surely understand that I don't wish to hear you confirm what I already know.'

'Embarrass me!' he invited harshly. 'Embarrassment will be an entirely new experience.'

'Please, Ramón! I know about Consuelo! Don't play games with me!'

She turned tear-filled eyes on him and he drew back and rested against the dressing-table, his arms folded across his chest, his eyes as shuttered as they had ever been.

'How do you know about Consuelo? She is miles away!'

So he was confirming it. Her last hopes died.

'Your aunt came today. She told me—she told me that Consuelo can never have children. She—she told me that an heir was needed and that I was the sacrifice because—because you wanted me in any case.' Her eyes fell and she stared unseeing at the deep carpet knowing that she could not go on for much longer. The strain had been too much. Nausea was beginning to well up inside her and her skin felt clammy and cold. 'I rang to tell you, hoping it wasn't true, but you were at the house, the other house. You were there with Consuelo!'

She turned and raced to the bathroom slamming the door, her whole body racked with the bitter sickness of pregnancy, tension and grief. For a few minutes she stood on the point of fainting, blackness washing over her, receding and then returning as she clutched tightly to the edge of the mirror.

Then Ramón was there, wiping her face with a cool cloth, forcing a little water between her trembling lips and lifting her gently into his arms. She was too spent to struggle and he also was white as a sheet.

He sat in an armchair, settling her on his lap, her head lifeless against his shoulder, and it was comfort, security, happiness, but she struggled weakly to be free. This was not now for her and she did not want his tender affection.

'Stay with me,' he begged, his voice uneven. 'Let us face this nightmare together.' His arms tightened around her. 'At this moment I could destroy the whole Ortiga clan but they can wait. Now there is you and I. There is also the truth.'

'I don't want to hear the truth!' She struggled up, her hand again on her stomach, clinging to what was real like a charm to ward off evil, and he subdued her easily with no harshness whatever, his eyes following the movement of her hand, making her flush and snatch her hand away.

'This is the—heir you were sacrificed to produce?' he asked quietly. 'I should perhaps remind you that there is already an heir, your beloved Manolito. My father had foreseen the possibility of any difficulties and I would say without doubt that your mother was the sacrifice, because I can tell you without any question that although she was a decorative companion he never ceased to love my own mother. When she died he turned to stone, the inheritance and its security his only reason for living. Inez, it appeared, was perfectly willing to be the sacrifice in order to have wealth and ease. A sacrifice of that nature was never required of you. You were required to sacrifice something very different: your country, your father, your own way of life.' His hand came to take the place of hers, flat and warm on her stomach, possessive and gentle with a touch that sent flames through her whole being. 'This is not an—heir, Meriel. This is a baby, our child, and there is only one reason why it is there.' He looked into the wide grey eyes as he had looked since she was a child, his gaze roaming across her tear-starred lashes, her wet cheeks, her trembling mouth. 'I love you,' he said softly. 'I have never dared to say it before, never felt that I had the right to place such a burden on you, but now it must be said and you must choose your own sacrifice whether to stay with me or go away knowing how I feel.'

For a second she closed her eyes, unable to take any more emotion, unwilling to believe the evidence of her own ears, but when she opened them he was leaning over her, his face tender and wistful, his eyes burning into hers.

'Ramón!' She shook her head, unable to grasp the

happiness that had been so quietly handed to her, and she saw his smile, long and slow as his hand moved warmly and gently over the place that she instinctively protected.

'I love you, my sweet and adorable Meriel,' he whispered. 'My clever little wife, the reason for my days, the joy of my nights. If you leave me then it must be with the knowledge of this and with the knowledge that were I to live for ever there would be nobody else in my heart, no other woman at the *hacienda* of the Ortigas, no other wife for me, and I would be like the rocks that rise from the plains, cold and hard, lonely and silent, with just memories to keep me alive.'

CHAPTER TEN

FOR a second only Meriel met Ramón's eyes, seeing the wistful longing there, the great love he had never allowed her to see, and then she wound her arms tightly around his neck, holding on until he gasped and laughed shakily, his arms closing round her like a fortress of warmth.

'I love you, Ramón!' she cried, tears, laughter and happiness mixed up on her face as he took her hand gently in his hands and looked down at her.

'I know,' he smiled, his voice deep and gentle. 'I know that you love me. I have known since you were little more than sixteen. I saw awe and admiration turn to something much more tangible, much more durable. It came into my mind to keep you here when you were seventeen and describing to me the way you had mapped out your future in England.' He laughed at her surprise and shook her head gently. 'At that moment I developed an intense dislike for all things Anglo-Saxon,' he confessed wryly. 'When you did not come at Christmas I had to use every ounce of self-discipline not to get on to a plane and fetch you here by your long yellow hair. When you did come,' he added softly, 'I lost my head in a few moments in the moonlight.'

'Why did you send me away?' she whispered, her hand stroking his face as he gathered her against him tenderly.

'You were too young,' he stated simply. 'You were warm, alive, willing and the greatest temptation of my life, but inside, you were afraid. I knew you as I know myself and I knew that I would have to let you go, hoping that the love would grow and not fade into a dream and die. It was the hardest thing I have ever had to do.'

'I thought you were in love with Consuelo,' she confessed against his shoulder, and felt his silent laughter, but his

175

voice was tinged with a remembered bitterness when he answered.

'I know. I realised that I was hurting you, but in this I thought I would save you from a greater and more permanent hurt.' He paused for a moment and her heart gave a frightening lurch. She knew that the moment had come when she would learn about Consuelo and she had not yet fully grasped her new-found happiness sufficiently for any hurts to slide easily away.

'By the time that you were eighteen,' he said quietly, 'I knew Consuelo very well. For a whole year I did not see you and I fought against a desire that was in many ways unacceptable to me. I could not make the adjustment from one kind of love to another. Duty has always been strong in me and I had seen you as a duty, one who needed my protection as Manuel needed it. Consuelo and I saw a great deal of each other. She is closer to my own age, easy to get on with, and she is very charming,' he sighed and held her close,' but it was of very little use. Your face was always before me and I could not learn to love anyone else. She was a good friend, though, and we were never lovers.'

She lifted grey eyes to meet the burning darkness of his and saw, as she had always seen, only the truth written there. Whatever he had to tell her mattered not at all now, he loved her and nothing else mattered.

'Did she know about—about me?' Meriel ventured softly.

'Everything about you,' he confessed with a laugh. 'She was the only one that I could tell, and I wanted to speak about you even if only to hear your name spoken. She, too, needed a friend and I am glad that I have been able to be that.'

'Why were you with her at that house?' She sat up and looked at him, seeing the rueful twist of his perfect lips as he answered.

'An act of kindness that almost lost me the one who is everything in my life,' he answered. 'Consuelo is also in love, has been in love for years. The man is not, however, of a wealthy family, and her father is, as you have no doubt seen, a man who gives not one inch when his own interests are at stake. The man was the manager at the Sandoval mine. He is the best mining engineer in Venezuela, we would all have paid him anything to have him in our employ but he would not move, because of Conseulo. Only there at the Sandoval mine did he have any chance of seeing her at all.

'Soon after you returned to me, he declared his love and the matter was put to Señor Sandoval. The action he took was typical of him; he fired his manager and forbade Consuelo to see him again. The night before our wedding his deeds rebounded on him, he had a strike on his hands and he came to my study to beg me to help. While I have been away this week, I have helped, I have persuaded the men back to work and they were willing as soon as they knew the fate of their greatly respected manager.'

'What happened to him? What is Consuelo going to do?' Now that she knew everything, Meriel's instincts were to assist Consuelo. In this day and age it seemed monstrous that anyone could cause another such unhappiness because of wealth.

'She is going to marry him, my love,' Ramón said softly, 'and you,' he added, tilting her chin, 'are to attend her; she especially wishes it.'

'Oh! I'm so glad!' Meriel suddenly laughed and looked at him with devilment. 'That's one in the eye for your aunt!'

'I will deal with Doña Barbara,' he said darkly. 'First we will settle our differences, then we will get Consuelo married and then—Tia Barbara!'

'What will they do, though?' Meriel asked worriedly. 'I mean with no job, no home . . .'

'Did I not tell you that he was the best mining engineer in Venezuela?' Ramón said with a grin.' He is working for us, love of my life. If Señor Sandoval can see his way to reason and bless the marriage then perhaps we will allow

him to borrow our manager from time to time if he runs
into any trouble. As to a home, I have given them the other
Ortiga house; that is why I was there with Consuelo. You
are not jealous of that, or worried?'

'No, you're very generous and kind.' She wound her
arms around his neck and for long moments was lost in the
love that was poured over her by the dark and vibrant
being who held her as close as death, his arms her only
refuge in life as they had always been.

'I think, though,' she accused when he released her, 'that
you could have telphoned me. I've been so cut off from you.'

'When I am away I cannot telephone you,' he confessed.
'I learned that when I started to telephone you on my odd
days away when we came back from our honeymoon. The
mere sound of your voice and everything else leaves my
head. I hear your voice and I want you. The only thing I
can think of is getting back. It is your gentleness that comes
out on the telephone, I hear it even when you are angry as
you were angry when I phoned you in England, and also
there is your delicious little accent.'

'I speak Spanish fluently!' she protested. 'I have no
accent whatsoever.'

'You speak it beautifully and with great ease,' he
admitted soothingly. 'Much better than I speak English,
but still there is that delightful little accent, and I would not
like you to lose it. It is so sexy!'

'Ramón! How can you say that!'

'Ramón!' he mocked. 'How can you say that! You are
doing it now, beloved, and it is turning my bones to water.
Come, let us walk out in the garden before I start to get
other ideas. I have been away for two weeks and my self-
discipline is very slack at the moment.'

They walked in the gathering cool of the garden, arms
around each other, and there was a contentment in Meriel
that there had never been before.

'If only you had told me you loved me long ago,' she
sighed as his arms held her close. 'I would never have gone

back to England. I would have waited here until you wanted to marry me.'

'I know that,' he assured her. 'I knew that then. One day, though, you might have wondered what it would have been like to live in England, to have a corner of your own, to see more of your father, and I would then have seen it in your eyes and it would have been a grief to both of us. You had to fly by yourself, soar in your own freedom, learn where your heart truly rested.'

'You never called me at all, never wrote,' she whispered, remembering her earlier despair when she had first left Venezuela.

'Freedom is not freedom when there is a rein on it,' he said deeply, turning her into his arms. 'No matter how tender and loving the rein, no matter how loosely held, it tethers you to the past and I wanted your future, freely given.'

'How did you get to be so clever?' she asked, smiling lovingly into his eyes.

'It is a matter of birth,' he said with mocking arrogance. 'I was born like that, you will have to work at it.'

Her tussle with him was broken short as they felt the first drops of rain and both turned their faces to the sky and the distant mountains now black with storm warnings.

'At last it is here,' he sighed happily. 'The rains are coming, the dry and the dust are over and everything will renew itself and become green and filled with life. When next the land is dry I will have a son of my own!'

He lifted her into his arms holding her high against him, his face filled with a glorious happiness as he carried her back towards the room they had left a short while ago, placing her on her feet and drawing the curtains.

'What are you doing?' she asked, startled as the room became dim and mysterious, the light faint.

'You are afraid of the *tormenta*,' he reminded her, the flash of his teeth white as he smiled wickedly. 'I am shutting it out.'

'It's only rain,' she protested, 'and not much of that yet.'

He stood perfectly still, listening, his eyes a dark gleam in the dimness of the room, and she heard, far away, the first roll of thunder, her hand going to her mouth in instant anxiety.

'You know that there is nothing to fear,' he said softly coming towards her, 'You know I will not leave you. The curtains are drawn, the door is locked and I love the storms and the darkness, they first drove you to my arms.'

She moved into his arms now, as eager as he to be lost in their own kind of storm, hearing his quiet grumbles as he undressed her.

'What is it?' she laughed as he held her away, exasperation on his face.

'When I undress you, I like it to be easy,' he murmured. 'I like you to be able to stay close to me the whole time. More than that also I do not like trousers. I like to see your long and slender legs.' He slid the white trousers from her hips and lifted her into his arms, his elegant toe kicking them aside. 'We will have a ceremonial burning of those,' he asserted grimly.

'They're silk!' she protested, hiding her face against him as the first flash of lightning lit the room.

'So are you, my darling,' he breathed, placing her on the bed, his hands running with the familiarity of possession over her as he came to take her in his arms, 'and now there are no shadows between us. I can show you how I feel, how I love you.'

There was no postponing his hunger and Meriel felt the same way too. She had thought that she had lost him, thought that she would have to leave this house, this land and the man who made her life heaven, and her response had his breath catching in his throat.

They came together with a passionate ferocity that seemed to soar over the ferocity of the storm that raged outside, and she did not notice the violence of sound that the thunder brought as she listened to the thunder of his heart over her own. The dazzling lights that shone before her were inside her own head as they climbed beyond the world, lost in a timeless world of their own.

'You are enchantment,' he whispered huskily as she lay still and content beneath him at last. 'You are everything that I have dreamed of. You give me more than any man could ever hope for, and when you call my name in that little cry of passion it is with that delicate, sexy little accent.'

'And your bones melt,' she teased, breathlessly, her fingers tracing his smiling lips.'

'Repeatedly,' he whispered, capturing her hand and kissing each finger lingeringly.

'Manolito is not home yet,' she told him worriedly as he moved to the side and drew her into his arms. She found that she could watch the lightning flare across the sky with no fear whatever and that the sound of the thunder was merely interesting. 'You've cured me of my fear of storms,' she said excitedly, coming up on one elbow and looking at him with astonishmemnt.

'I hope not,' he said lazily. 'I want more time to work on the cure, do not be too hasty. We will certainly have to put in more time on the kind of therapy that you need.' He pulled her across him, laughing into her face, no trace of the dark silence she had known for so long on the beloved face that adored her.

'As to Manolito,' he said darkly, 'he is with Señor Morales and quite safe. Do not make me jealous,' he added, biting gently at her neck.

'What about Manolito?' she asked when the tender assault was over and she lay relaxed and content beside him. 'I mean, what about the inheritance?'

'I have already taken steps about that,' he assured her seriously. 'When I discovered your ability to absorb the business side of things I put into action plans that I made long ago. A block of shares in the estate has been transferred to you. You may now attend the meetings and speak your mind, throw your slender weight about,' he added, his hand sliding over her seductively. 'It is time that the family recognised that there is a new and dynamic Ortiga among them.'

'Oh, Ramón, I don't think . . .'

'I do!' he asserted forcefully. 'You are too clever and talented to sit about here and do nothing.'

'Well, there'll be the baby . . .' she began but he was not to be put off.

'You will manage that beautifully as well,' he assured her with pride in his voice, 'And there will be more than one. This one has filled me with so much joy that I can see no way that it will not be having company very quickly. As to Manuel, I have split the inheritance down the middle; he is also my father's son. Until he is of age, we will guard his inheritance and then he will take up the burden on his own. One day he too will have children and with ours and his, the Ortiga wealth will be split into a normal share of prosperity, not this deadly weight that both my father and I have carried for so many years. Should we both have children who will spend it unwisely, then one day it will cease to exist.'

'Wouldn't you care about that?' she gasped, the calmness of his announcement stunning her.

'What I care about, all that I have cared about for many, many years, I hold now in my arms,' he said seriously. 'The rest is duty, a mere burden that I bear.'

'Do I deserve you?' she asked, looking at him with a glowing adoration that had the dark eyes gleaming into hers.

'Probably not,' he assured her with laughter in his voice, but then his teasing stopped suddenly. 'I have not forgotten how you have been hurt,' he said angrily. 'Today we will love and celebrate our new happiness. Tomorrow I shall get to Tia Barbara!'

'She's not important,' Meriel sighed, kissing the suddenly tight lips.

'This much she is about to find out,' Ramón promised darkly.

It was only later when they sat to a happy and candlelit dinner with Manuel, the generator having failed again and the storm returned with a vengeance, that Ramón put forth his final plan.

Manuel had entertained them for most for the meal with his many small but interesting adventures, congratulating himself and not Señor Morales that they had managed to arrive back between the storms, and Señor Morales had been able to return to his own home in good time.

'I did not know until he told me at our wedding that your father was an accountant,' Ramón said, looking closely at Meriel. 'It is odd, when he has meant so much to you, that I didn't even know what he did for a living.'

'There was a time,' she said quietly, 'when I found it a little painful even to talk about him. Since then, well . . .'

Ramón's hand came to cover hers, his outright adoration bringing a pleased gleam to Manuel's eyes, their liquid darkness taking in everything.

'I had wondered,' Ramón said gently, 'if he would like to come here and work for the Oritga Estates. It would take a great deal of work from my shoulders,' he added hastily as she gasped. 'I could really do with him here.'

'You are really the most wonderful person in the whole world,' Meriel said softly, wishing for once that Manolito were in his own room so that she could show Ramón how she felt. He knew, however, because a slow burn of heat spread across his cheek-bones as she looked at him and his hand tightened on hers.

'You have plenty of accountants,' she reminded him softly, 'and I don't need my father under my watchful eye. In any case, he wouldn't come. He has his own firm; it's small and not rich but they do a good deal of business and they have a respected name. Also,' she added, her eyes twinkling, 'I really think that there's a certain lady . . .'

'Ah!' Ramón looked at her intently. 'You do not mind?'

'Darling!' she laughed delightedly. 'Why should I mind? Let's leave him to get on with his own life at last. He'll have to put up with hearing my—voice on the phone.'

'Ah! You will be speaking in English, it is not the same.' Ramón laughed, his eyes teasingly on her.

'It is a great pity,' Manuel cut in, no longer able to hold his tongue. 'I am greatly fond of Señor Curtis. What relation is he to me?' he added turning to Meriel.

'I wonder sometimes if you are in full possession of your faculties,' Ramón murmured, returning to his coffee. 'I would have thought that you had enough relatives already without this insatiable desire to claim more.'

'I'd like a few that I can be happy about,' Manuel said mutinously, his eyes suddenly worried when he caught the wryly amused look on Ramón's face, the dark raised eyebrows that had so troubled Meriel when she was his age. 'I'm sorry, Ramón,' he apologised quickly, relaxing when he saw Ramón's quick grin.

'I really understand your feelings,' Ramón assured him seriously, his laughter quickly suppressed. 'However, take note: the only Ortigas who matter are right here in this room; the others will, I think be keeping well away in the future, the more—gloomy ones,' he added with a smile at Meriel that threw her headlong into the past.

Later in their room, Meriel asked the question that had been hovering on her lips all evening.

'Why didn't you tell Manolito about the baby?' she asked, her face carefully hidden as she undressed for bed.

'I'm damned if I'll share everything with my brother,' he growled, his hands warm on her skin as he dealt with the zip of her dress. 'Why didn't you tell him, if you are anxious for him to know?'

'I'm not,' she murmured, her lashes covering her eyes as he turned her slowly towards him.' It's a glorious secret that I only want to share with you.'

'Those words have cured me of my tiny bit of jealousy,'

he smiled, kissing her eyes closed and easing her into his arms. 'Secrets with you are my greatest joy.'

'Rosita will tell him,' she sighed, but Ramón laughed, his breath fanning her hair.

'She will not!' he said with a certainty.' He frequently complains that she thinks he is only a boy.'

Their laughter mingled as his lips found hers and he lifted her up into his arms, smiling into her loving eyes.

'I sometimes wonder,' she mused as she lay watching him getting ready for bed, 'what would have happened if there had not been that dreadful accident. It's very sad to me that it took such a tragedy to get us together again.'

He stood still and looked down at her, his shirt still in his hand, his lean body dark and gleaming in the light of the lamps that had now returned to lighten the room with soft colour, his narrow hips powerful and graceful in the black trousers he had worn for dinner.

She wished she had not voiced such a melancholy thought to spoil their joy and happiness, but Ramón simply watched her for a minute and then moved to the small drawer of the bedside table and felt inside.

'This would have happened,' he said quietly, handing her an airline ticket that was very much out of date. She glanced at the date, March, the destination London, and her eyes searched his face in a kind of wonder.

'I was waiting for their return,' he said softly, sitting beside her and lifting her into his arms. 'I had listened for three years to every word that Inez spoke of you. She was so proud. You were doing well, a success, tackling a difficult and demanding job with a flair she had not recognised you possessed. She was delighted, too, with Mackensie and your—glittering life-style. The London scene for the rising and brilliant Miss Curtis. Nights in beautiful ball-gowns with the giant Señor Mackensie at your side. Every word she spoke made me die a little. It was what I had dreaded, the reason I had let you go free; it was happening and I could not stop myself from listening. I had nothing to offer that would replace it. There were the days in the house, the trips to Caracas, the vast stretches of the plains to hem you into the gloom you had discovered here.' He sighed and wiped a tear that had come unbidden to her eyes and trailed slowly down the soft glow of her cheek. 'I loved you so very much and I was torn apart. Finally I decided to come and see for myself how you felt, although I had really no hope. I imagined that after nearly seven years you would have forgotten. I imagined that you would be in love with Mackensie. In the event, I never came. The plane bringing them back crashed and I found myself once again chained by duty. I can only thank God that you came to me.'

'Ramón! Ramón!' She pressed close to him, raining kisses on his face, frantic tiny caresses that had his lips urgently searching for hers. 'I never stopped loving you. I told myself that I'd got over it but I knew that I hadn't.'

'Mackensie said you hated me,' he accused gently, his arms tightening around her.

'I had to tell myself that,' she whispered. 'I thought I'd never see you again, never hear your voice, never feel your kisses, and Mother spoke of you too, always in connection with Consuelo. I thought that it was a part of my life that was over and would haunt me for ever.'

'You would have married Mackensie?' he asked fiercely, looking down at her.

'No. I would have been a fast-talking, hard-headed salesperson, just as you said so long ago. A bitter one. I would never have recovered from loving you.'

'I don't want you to recover,' he whispered fiercely against her ear, his arms crushing her to him, 'because I shall never recover from loving you. It is an illness that we shall live with happily for the rest of our lives.'

He moved over her, his love strong and real, and her hands went limp, her body turned to melting flame, her last act to crush the airline ticket and allow it to fall from her languid hand. They would never need to fly to each other.

They would never be apart again. It was a love that had flowered in silence, had grown over the years and changed to a burning passion that distance had only fanned into a brilliant flame. Nothing could separate them now because they knew each other like two halves of the same mould.

'Ramón!' she whispered and felt his lips smile against her skin at the sound of his name on her lips.

'Say that again, my sweet, beautiful love and I shall feel my bones turn to water before I devour your sweetness.'

He felt the smile on her lips too as his arms drew her closer.

'Ramón!' she whispered, 'I love you.' Try as she might she could hear no accent, but he heard and his face lifted to hers, his smile sensuous and tempting.

'My beautiful English rose,' he murmured in English, the soft accent turning her heart over, widening her eyes. 'You see?' he murmured. 'It is a game that two can play. If ever I am away again I shall ring you several times a day and we will converse in English. That way you will take the full brunt of the temptation. You must learn to share the responsibility now that you are grown up.' His smiling lips captured hers and no further words were necessary.

Harlequin American Romance

Romances that go one step farther...
American Romance

Realistic stories involving people you can relate to and
care about.

Compelling relationships between the mature men and
women of today's world.

Romances that capture the core of genuine emotions
between a man and a woman.

Join us each month for four new titles wherever paperback
books are sold.
Enter the world of American Romance.

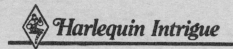

Harlequin Presents

COMING NEXT MONTH

1087 MY BROTHER'S KEEPER Emma Goldrick
Mickey is over the moon to have Harry home again. Life is good with her stepbrother around. Yet it's strange that she finds her thoughts centering less on her fiancé, George, and more on Harry....

1088 JENNY'S TURN Vanessa Grant
Making award-winning documentaries with Jake has been fun! However, when he declares his intention to marry her best friend, Jenny decides to leave. She'll never be one of Jake's women, but she can't stand the thought of him marrying someone else!

1089 FIGHT FOR LOVE Penny Jordan
When Natasha makes friends with an old Texas rancher in London, she never dreams that one day he'll leave her a legacy in his will. It isn't until she's at his ranch near Dallas that she begins to guess at his motives.

1090 FRAZER'S LAW Madeleine Ker
Rio enjoys studying the marine life off Australia's untamed Cape York Peninsula. She resents the intrusion of biologist Cameron Frazer into her remote solitude. But having to fight danger together makes her realize just how much they have in common.

1091 WHEN LOVERS MEET Flora Kidd
Jilly couldn't say that Ed Forster hadn't warned her. He'd made it very clear from the start that he wasn't interested in commitment. Recently widowed Jilly, however, isn't ready for a "torrid tropical affair"!

1092 NO MAN'S MISTRESS Roberta Leigh
A woman would have to be a real man-hater not to appreciate Benedict Peters—and Sara is no man-hater. Just the same she isn't going to join the admiring throng that sits at his feet—no matter how persuasive he is!

1093 REASONS OF THE HEART Susan Napier
Meeting Ross Tarrant brings Francesca's adolescent humiliation back with a jolt. Older and wiser now, successful in her way of life—surely she'll have the upper hand over the seemingly lackadaisical Ross. It just doesn't work out that way, though.

1094 DISHONOURABLE INTENTIONS Sally Wentworth
Rex Kynaston has everything it takes to attract a woman. The trouble is, he knows it. Not that it matters to Harriet. As far as she's concerned, he's the last man on earth she'd get involved with....

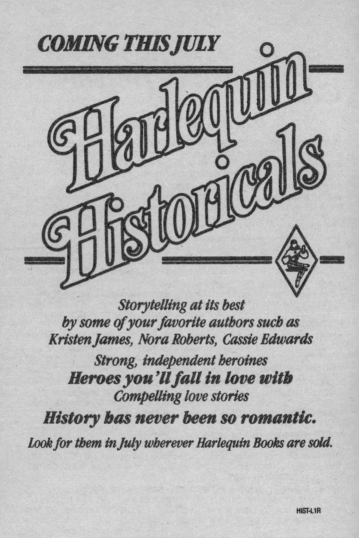

COMING THIS JULY

Harlequin Historicals

*Storytelling at its best
by some of your favorite authors such as
Kristen James, Nora Roberts, Cassie Edwards*

Strong, independent heroines
Heroes you'll fall in love with
Compelling love stories

History has never been so romantic.

Look for them in July wherever Harlequin Books are sold.